# Son of the Dragon

## (Sons of Beasts, Book 3)

### T. S. JOYCE

# Son of the Dragon

ISBN-13: 978-1976493461
ISBN-10: 1976493463
Copyright © 2017, T. S. Joyce
First electronic publication: September 2017

T. S. Joyce
www. tsjoyce.com

All Rights Are Reserved. No part of this book may be used or reproduced in any manner whatsoever without written permission, except in the case of brief quotations embodied in critical articles and reviews. The unauthorized reproduction or distribution of this copyrighted work is illegal. No part of this book may be scanned, uploaded or distributed via the Internet or any other means, electronic or print, without the author's permission.

NOTE FROM THE AUTHOR:

This book is a work of fiction. The names, characters, places, and incidents are products of the writer's imagination or have been used fictitiously and are not to be construed as real. Any resemblance to persons, living or dead, actual events, locale or organizations is entirely coincidental. The author does not have any control over and does not assume any responsibility for third-party websites or their content.

Published in the United States of America

First digital publication: September 2017
First print publication: September 2017

Editing: Corinne DeMaagd
Cover Photography: Wander Aguiar
Cover Model: Tyler Halligan

# DEDICATION

For 1010.

# ACKNOWLEDGMENTS

I couldn't write these books without some amazing people behind me. A huge thanks to Corinne DeMaagd, for helping me to polish my books, and for being an amazing and supportive friend. Looking back on our journey here, it makes me smile so big. You are an incredible teammate, C!

Thanks to Tyler Halligan, the cover model for this book and a few of my others. Any time I get the chance to work with him, I take it because he has always been a great friend to me. #TnT. Thank you to Wander Aguiar and his amazing team for this shot for the cover. You always get the perfect image for what I'm needing.

And last but never least, thank you, awesome reader. You have done more for me and my stories than I can even explain on this teeny page. You found my books, and ran with them, and every share, review, and comment makes release days so incredibly special to me.

1010 is magic and so are you.

# ONE

"Don't be scared," Emmitt murmured over his shoulder.

Riyah Mercer clutched her clipboard closer to her chest and smiled at the back of the security guard's thinning hair. That was so nice of him to care—

"Because they'll sense that fear and kill you."

Oh.

The smile fell from her lips as a massive silverback shifter slammed his entire body against one of the cell doors. The bars gonged with the force. The low noise faded when he paced away, but then he turned and charged the bars again. Gong! This time he stayed, huge hands wrapped around the bars, his eyes totally empty and staring right through her.

Emmitt gave a quick flick of his fingers. "You'll get used to that. He's been doing it for a month straight. That's Titus."

"I don't think it's healthy for him to be caged up like that then," she said, unable to keep her eyes from the giant.

"Murdered three people in their sleep. Humans. Still feel sorry for him?"

Riyah swallowed bile and ripped her gaze away from the insane animal. The next cage held a man as tall as a building and covered in tattoos, with a feral smile for her as she passed. He spat at the floor right by her shoes and uttered something deplorable about what he was going to do to her body so he could listen to her scream.

She scurried to catch up to Emmitt's long strides.

"Look," he muttered. "I'll be completely honest. I voted against you."

"What?"

"A woman don't belong in this hell. That's what this is, Mercer. It's hell. The inmates here? They aren't what you are used to dealing with at your last prison. They are monsters, and they will slit your throat the second they get the chance. Do you know how many casualties have come with this job?"

"I don't want to know."

"Seventeen since this facility opened three years ago. All humans. All strong men who were trained in combat, trained to subdue the demons who live in these walls. Even now, you don't realize it, but you're being hunted." Emmitt's gaze bore into her as he jammed a finger at a larger cell with an enormous lion pacing in front of the bars, his gold eyes never leaving her. "Meet one of the dominants of the Dunn Pride. He's set to be released next week. He'll come after me and the other guards, and after you the second they let him out. He's been here three times now. He always hunts the guards. A snapped Dunn lion? He can't even help hunting us. Three strikes, and he's out."

"What does that mean?"

"Means we get to finally put that fucker down. His pride refused to do the dirty work, so it's on us now."

"Put him down? Like…kill him?"

Emmitt sighed as he slid his master key card into a reader on the wall. "I can tell you won't last a day here. Your sympathy for these animals will get you hurt or worse. Like I said. I voted against you, but this was the higher-ups' decision. They're desperate, and you're the Hail Mary. Lucky fuckin' you. You're gonna burn to ashes for this job."

Her hands shook so bad she clutched her clipboard tighter. She could do this. She had to. There was no choice. When Clara Daye asked a person to do the impossible, they did it. Or they died trying. Because she was the mother of the Red Dragon, and only Clara and Riyah knew what she was really doing here. Not even Damon Daye, the Blue Dragon himself, knew what his mate was up to. Clara Daye was good and done letting her mate run this show, and she'd just taken control without anyone in Damon's Mountains knowing. She'd done it quick, too. She'd approached Riyah last week, and look, here she was, seven days later, with a high-clearance job at the most secure shifter prison in the world, on her way to the underground bowels of hell, as Emmitt had so eloquently called it, to sit in a room with the most terrifying creature on the entire planet.

And what was wrong with her? She wasn't scared of Vyr, like she should be. No, she was scared of failing. Scared of the monsters behind her, but not the one below her.

If this was hell, then Vyr Daye was the devil himself, and she would be meeting him within minutes.

Maybe she was in shock. Or perhaps she was shut down because of the whirlwind of the last week, but she only half-listened to Emmitt explain how to use her card to get down to the lower levels where they kept "the evil ones," as the old guard called them.

Evil. That word... Riyah had seen real evil, and so far, none of the shifters she'd passed gave off those vibes. Emmitt's definition was probably vastly different from her own.

A week ago, she'd quit the prison she'd worked for the last year, packed up her life, and moved to the Arizona desert to likely die by fire, like Emmitt had said. She felt numb as the elevator took them deeper and deeper underground. The temperature changed gradually, growing colder and colder until gooseflesh raised across her forearms.

"Bring a jacket next time. They keep it cold down here for the dragon. He's like a snake. The cold slows him down. If it gets too warm, he's even harder to manage. He thrives in heat. He withers in cold. We learned that little trick with Dark Kane."

Riyah snapped back to attention at the mention of the End of Days. "You worked with the Black Dragon?"

"Call him what he is, Mercer. Apocalypse. Vyr is even worse. Not for long, though."

She shook her head, utterly baffled. "Dark Kane was never in shifter prison. How did you work with him?"

"Not with him. I worked on him. You signed the confidentiality agreement. You utter a word outside of these walls, and your entire life will be set on fire. This place is shifter prison. This place is also how we fix the baddies. It's also a research facility." The elevator made a hideous buzzing noise and the doors opened. The sterile white hallway split in two. Emmitt pointed down the right tunnel. "Research. We'll tour the New IESA lab after your interview. Boss says it's imperative you get that done today. So far, Vyr has refused to talk to anyone. It makes things...difficult." He gestured to follow him down the left hallway. "This hall is what we call the highway to hell. And since you have a sympathy problem, we're making a pitstop."

They passed several thick glass cells with shifters,

all in human form. She had no guess what their animals were, but now she was sensing the darkness that Emmitt hinted at. The baddies. These were deemed the worst, hidden down here away from the rest of the world for its protection.

The hall seemed to stretch for eternity as her heels clacked neatly on the tile, echoing with each step she took. Twice, Emmitt gave her shoes a narrow-eyed sideways glance. "Please don't wear victim shoes to work anymore. You can't run in those."

"I'm not a guard. I'm a counselor, and this place is secure, right? Why would I need to run?"

"Seventeen," Emmitt murmured, sliding his card at a security panel beside a door. He shoved it open and glared at her as she passed through. "Don't matter who you are down here. The second you forget that number, you'll become eighteen."

The room was dark, but as they entered the small space, the lights clicked on by a sensor. There was a desk covered in notes, a computer, security screens, and an empty Cheetos package. Through the window, the lights in a cavernous room came on, too. And sitting there on a bare mattress, on an iron bed, surrounded by black scorch marks, the Red Dragon himself stared back at the glass—right at her.

She stood there frozen, unable to move a single muscle, as if ensnared in a cobra's stare. He looked so different from the man she'd seen on the news, from the pictures Clara had sent of him as a boy and a young adult. His red hair was burred close to the scalp, and he wore a plain white shirt that clung to the defined muscles of his broad shoulders and chest. Tattoo ink peeked out from under the sleeve, decorating his tensed bicep on his left arm. He looked pale, and there was a long, fresh scar that ran from his temple back, back, disappearing behind his head. There was no greeting smile on his lips. In fact, there were no smile lines around his mouth, as if the man had never smiled a day in his life. His cheeks were hollow, and he had bags under his eyes. Even wrecked, he was the most striking man she'd ever seen, and her heart banged against her chest as she realized why he looked so demolished. It was his eyes.

One was the color of a summer sky, and the other was silver with an elongated pupil.

Her chest physically hurt.

Fuck the New IESA and fuck what they were doing to Vyr. She wanted to puke. Eventually, they would take his dragon. They would kill him, and that beast would be still and dead inside him. Both his eyes would freeze and remain silver with those reptilian pupils, as if his dragon was a staring corpse inside him.

Her chest heaved as she fought to gain control of her emotions for Emmitt. Right now, she wanted to kill him. Riyah wasn't violent by nature, but she already felt like she knew Vyr because she knew his mother, who loved him like he was the sun and the moon. This was a man born with a monster in him. Not his fault. He was being tortured for something he had no control over. Her eyes stung, and she blinked hard. Clearing her throat, she carefully asked, "Why was he sitting in the dark? And if you're so concerned about what a beast he is, why is there no one in here watching him?"

"He is a creature of darkness, Mercer. He's comfortable there."

"Yeah, the goddamn scorch marks all over the walls back your theory."

"Seventeen is sitting in the belly of the beast."

"W-what?" she asked, ripping her attention from the man.

Emmitt made his way to the computer and brought the screen to life. "No one is in here observing because this is my office. There are two more across the way. Those have someone in them at all times. We didn't leave the Red Dragon alone. It's against the rules to not have at least two rooms occupied at all times in case he goes off the rails again."

"Again," she repeated, her gaze drifting back to Vyr. He looked harmless enough, just sitting there with his fists clenched between his knees. Just to test, she moved a few steps to the side, and his gaze followed her.

"Can he see me?"

"No. This is two-way glass. He sees his own reflection." Emmitt looked up from his screen at Vyr. Quick as a whip, the dragon shifter with the vacant eyes turned his head to the left. Huh. So Emmitt didn't realize Vyr could sense them. When Emmitt gave his attention to the glowing computer screen again, Vyr blinked slowly and dragged his gaze directly back to her.

Chills rippled up her arms.

Clara had kept some things to herself, clearly. Riyah had a moment. She had a moment when she wondered if she'd been tricked into this, when she wondered at Clara's end game. Was Riyah at more risk than the red-haired grizzly shifter of Damon's Mountains had told her? She'd sworn up and down that Riyah would be safe with her son, but Vyr's gaze was filled with such fiery hatred, she was seriously questioning what the hell she was doing here.

"Here you go. I like to show this to all newbies as a warning." He stood back and let her have a better view of the video that was playing on the oversize monitor.

On it, a lone man approached Vyr, who looked cool and relaxed. At that point, his hair was shaved on the sides but longer on top. There wasn't a scar on his head. His eyes were piercing blue, and he was leaned back against the wall, one knee bent and his arm resting on it like he didn't have a care in the world. He smiled and seemed to say something cordially.

"What are they saying?" she asked.

"Don't know. There's no volume on this footage."

She was calling bullshit. There was volume—he

just wasn't letting her hear it. She had good instincts for when someone was lying. No, she wasn't a shifter, but she was something people here didn't know about or understand. Emmitt was stepping slowly to her bad side—a very unfortunate place to be.

Riyah set her clipboard down and locked her arms against the desk, squinted, and focused on the two men having a conversation on the grainy footage. Vyr clenched his fist once in the video, the muscles in his forearm flexing, but his face was still relaxed. He was even smiling. Sure, it looked like the devil's smile, but it still counted. He was talking now, his masculine lips forming words she would've given just about anything to hear.

Other than that clenched fist, nothing seemed off, and when he relaxed his hand, she naturally relaxed, too. Big mistake. With zero warning, a massive red dragon exploded from Vyr like a bomb going off. Fire covered the screen, and then there was the guard, burning. The Red Dragon opened his mouth, full of rows of razor sharp teeth, and the burning man disappeared into his maw. Vyr tossed his head back, swallowed, and lowered his gaze to the camera. He tensed and blasted fire onto it, and the screen went dark.

Utterly shocked, she stood there panting, traumatized, eyes glued to that black screen, wishing she could wash the memory of that awful few seconds from her mind.

Vyr really was a man-eater. A guiltless one. He was a monster, like Emmitt had said.

"Well, lookee there. You dropped your sympathy. Good. You'll live longer without it. Come on, Mercer."

"W-where are we going?"

Emmitt held open the door and smiled slowly. "You're going to meet the Red Dragon."

# TWO

Emmitt had definitely made her watch the video. Vyr didn't even try to swallow down the deep rumble of his dragon as Emmitt led the woman through the door.

Emmitt lifted the rifle and pulled the trigger. On reflex, Vyr caught the dart right before it slammed into his face. This was the part he hated with the burning passion of a thousand suns. This was the part where he tortured the best part of himself—the dragon. Keeping his face blank, he jammed the dart into his shoulder and emptied the contents. The pain was instant, the burn rocketing through every nerve ending in his body from the needle outward. Still, he sat there, staring at Emmitt like his body wasn't ripping apart.

This was the game. They could hurt him all they wanted, but he would never fuckin' show them a single grimace. He was dying, but he was doing it on his terms.

Fuck, he missed Torren. He'd never thought he would do this on his own. Never thought he would die in a cold room with strangers watching his every move. Never thought he would die in the dark without his best friend by his side. He even missed Nox, Nevada, and Candace. His dragon was inside of him, spewing blood, spewing fire, spewing pain and begging for one goddamn touch from any one of his crew, just to ease the hurt.

The bitter stench of the woman's fear filled his senses and made it even harder to control the Change. Fear made him want to kill things. It made him want to burn the world and be done with everything that was bad, and painful. It made him want to give into the growing darkness inside of him.

Emmitt left the woman alone and disappeared out the door. Just for a distraction from the pain, Vyr reached with his mind for her. Soft purple aura, and in her head was something beautiful. It was a memory. It was a small child's hand holding a bouquet of peonies. It swung back and forth. White dress. Field of dandelion flowers. Trailer park. Trailer. Stairs. Opening door. Old trailer with green carpet and holes in the walls, but he didn't get a feeling of hurt. She was happy, this girl child. She handed the flowers to a woman, and the smile on the woman's face lit up the room. And then Vyr was blasted backward out of the memory, out of the trailer, the door slamming shut as he hit the yard of dandelions. And then he was ripped from the woman's mind, and here he was again, in hell, burning from the inside out, looking at the pissed-off eyes of someone who truly confused him now.

"No," she said in a firm voice as if he was a puppy who had just pissed on the carpet.

What the fuck?

He saw her then…really studied her.

She looked different from any woman he'd ever seen. He had a light smattering of freckles on his face, a gift from his mother, but this woman had dark freckles that she hadn't covered with make-up. She displayed them proudly. She had dark, delicately arched eyebrows, a small elf nose, and eyes as black as midnight. Her lips were full, and her straight, brunette hair had been dyed blond at the ends. She was statuesque and curvy. She had that perfect hourglass figure that had the pain in his middle easing by a fraction as he dragged his attention down her body. There was something more about her. Something more than her being a rare beauty. Something he could sense, but couldn't put a finger on. Mysterious woman.

"What are you?" Vyr asked.

"Human," she answered easily.

Huh.

"Can I ask a favor?" she asked.

"I don't do interviews."

"That's not what I was going to ask."

A low rumble rattled through his body. "I have nothing to offer. Look around, human. I've been buried alive. Can't you see? You're asking favors of a dead man."

"Not a dead man. A half-dead dragon."

Vyr clenched his fists and barely resisted the urge to throw his bed against the wall just to quell the rage inside of him. Eyes closed, he counted to three and then locked his gaze on the woman. "What?" he snarled. "What could you possibly want from me?"

"I ask that you don't hurt me." Her eyes grew wider and her mouth set in a grim line. *I'm here to help you.*

The last part was a dream, right? Her lips hadn't moved, but the words were clear in his head. Vyr shook his head hard. He was at the beginning of The Sickening, and he'd been hearing and seeing things lately that weren't there. Too much time under the earth. Too long away from the sky. Too long in the dark. Too long away from his mountains.

Too long from his crew.

Emmitt had definitely shown her the video of him eating that prick guard, of him devouring a monster. Good for Emmitt. She should be wary of Vyr.

"I don't make promises I don't know I can keep. Sorry lady." He offered her an empty smile and tried to ignore the wave of nausea that wracked his body. Fuckin' meds were destroying him from the dragon out.

"Riyah."

"What?" Vyr asked.

"My name is Riyah Mercer. I'm going to be your counselor. I'm going to help you transition during this difficult time." She'd taken on a professional business voice, but her eyes flickered to the two-way glass of one of the observation rooms behind him.

*Help. Help... I'm here to help.*

Chills rippled up Vyr's arms, and he shook his head again hard. How many times had he sat here alone in the dark and fantasized about his crew coming through that wall and pulling him from this place? How many times had he wished for help? This woman, Riyah...she wasn't his crew. She wasn't going to save him. He was just going crazy with wanting.

Emmitt dragged in some video equipment.

"Fuck this," Vyr snarled, tensing up. "I'll take your goddamn meds, but I'm not letting you document the transition. Kill my dragon. That's the goal, right? But I'm not dying on camera."

"Settle," Riyah murmured so low, Emmitt didn't even react.

They both went to work, setting up a camera on a tripod. Vyr was gonna love the look on their faces when he crushed that fuckin' camera without even touching it. Anticipation grew in his middle, and he bit back a devilish smile. He rarely used his powers in front of other people, but fuck it all now, right? He was already dead. Vyr hoped it was expensive equipment. He was gonna let them get all set up, and then he was going to ruin their plans.

Emmitt adjusted the rifle on his shoulder and stood behind the chair he'd brought in for Riyah. "I'm ready when you are."

"This isn't happening with you in here," Riyah said in a firm voice.

Oh hoooo, feisty. God, it was awesome seeing Emmitt's stupid face go blank and then turn red in anger. Vyr didn't even hide his smile now. He wished he had popcorn.

"I'm not leaving you alone in here, Princess."

"Call me 'Princess' in front of the prisoners again, I dare you." Power was wafting from Riyah's skin in waves, and it amped Vyr up. What the fuck was she? Human, but more. Emmitt was full-on human with piddley little human senses, and he wasn't backing off Riyah like he should.

*Burn him. Burn. Him. Do it. Riyah, Riyah, she's on fiyah. Show me what you got, little lady.*

Vyr leaned forward on the edge of the mattress, body humming with power. "You heard her, Emmitt. Fuck off."

Emmitt's face was the color of Vyr's dragon scales now, and a chuckle bubbled up Vyr's throat. He flinched at the unfamiliar sound. A chuckle? He hadn't heard himself laugh in six months of being in shifter prison. Someday he was gonna eat Emmitt. He would laugh then, too.

"It's your funeral, Princess."

Riyah gave Vyr her back as she watched Emmitt walk out of the room and slam the metal door behind him. The noise echoed through the room. Well, that was fun, but he still wasn't going to let her record him.

Vyr ducked his face and ran his hands over his shaved head a few times to try to settle down. The nausea was back, and his organs felt like they were on fire. Riyah telling Emmitt to scram had just been a temporary relief. He was still here, still in the same dire situation. Only halfway through his year-long sentence, and he was losing his dragon too fast. He wasn't going to be able to save him. That much had become clear when one of his eyes froze with the dragon pupil and color last week. The same had happened to Dark Kane when they killed his dragon. The process was half-done. Fuck. He flinched at another wave of gut-wrenching pain.

"Your eye," Riyah whispered.

Plastering a smile on his face, he looked up at her. "You think it'll get me laid when I get out of here?"

Riyah sat slowly into the plastic chair and aimed the camera at him.

Vyr shook his head and ducked his gaze. He couldn't even look in the mirror. He sure as hell didn't want video of his dragon dying. He wanted to go out quietly, with his pride intact.

"You need to do this."

"I don't need to do anything."

"Is there volume on the monitors?"

Surprised by her question, he flickered his gaze to her and then back down. "Not when I don't want there to be." A quick, empty smile flickered across his face and disappeared before he murmured, "Scared yet?"

"Yes," she murmured. "Not of you, though. For you."

Vyr frowned. Her voice had stayed steady when she'd said it. "What the fuck is going on? Who are you?"

"I told you. I'm Riyah, the human."

"What time is it?"

"Why?"

"Are you a vampire?"

"No. I told you, I'm—"

"Yeah, yeah, human." Softly, he sang, "Secrets, secrets are no fun, unless you tell everyone."

"You wanna spill yours first then?"

Touché. "I'm still not doing this."

Riyah arched an eyebrow, and a red flashing light captured his attention. It was on the camera, but Riyah hadn't touched it. Hmmm.

With a snarl, he dropped his face in his hands and scrubbed them down. He hadn't slept well in six months and probably looked like hell. This video would likely be released to the public. "I don't want my mom to see me like this," he murmured. "I'm her only kid."

"I know. Can you state your full name?"

"I said I don't want to do interviews."

"Your father has requested this."

That was a lie. Her voice had faltered. Vyr hated liars. Maybe she was part of the New IESA too, just like all the assholes who came in here and took pieces of his skin, vials of his blood, who operated on him.

Maybe she was supposed to play good cop and get him to open up. Well, fuck that. He was dead inside, and no pretty face was going to change that.

Liar, liar, he hated liars. Why couldn't he read her mind? It pissed him off. Usually, he hated this part of his power. It dumped into everyone's mind, but right now he wanted it. He wanted to see her intentions because she was mixing him up. And even if his father had sent her? Vyr would still refuse this interview because Damon Daye was the one who had helped put him behind bars. He would feel his father's betrayal for the rest of his days. Vyr clenched his hands on his knees in a desperate attempt to soothe the sickly, raging dragon in his middle.

"What are your feelings after being here for six months?" she asked, looking down at a clipboard with her pen poised to write notes.

"I don't have feelings," Vyr said in a dead voice. "Never did." He wished he could see what she was writing.

"I've read your file and am aware you have had some issues with authority. What can this facility do to make this experience easier on you?"

"You mean what can they do to control me

better?"

"Sure."

Vyr ripped his gaze away from her and didn't answer. He wasn't giving them any more ammunition against him.

She tried again in a quieter, softer voice. "If you could have one thing here, for comfort, what would it be?"

Losing his damn mind, he uttered his only wish. "My crew." His voice broke on the last word. He missed them so fucking bad.

Riyah's voice dropped to a barely audible whisper. "They're trying to take your dragon. If you want to say something, request something, ask for help...do it now."

*Help. I'm here to help you, Vyr. Let me help. Clara. Clara. Clara Daye. I'm here because of Clara Daye.*

Vyr stared at his arms, stared at the gooseflesh that covered them. He never got cold. Okay. Maybe he was crazy. Maybe this was The Sickening. But that sounded like Riyah's voice in his head. She was reaching for him. He could feel it. Her chest was heaving now as she stared at him, and her eyes were rimmed with moisture. *Please*, she mouthed. She arched her eyebrows and nodded.

Mom sent Riyah to him? Fuck, fuck, fuck. He had to think. This was that little wisp of hope he'd been craving. She was offering it to him, right? But in here, he couldn't trust anyone. Not even if she claimed to be sent by his mother. Fuck. Think. She was offering him what? Help how? No one could help him stay steady, stay strong, except...

The Sons of Beasts. His crew.

Vyr swallowed hard and said, "Breaking and entering."

"What?" she asked.

"Vandalism. Illegal fights."

Vyr blinked slowly and locked his fiery gaze on the camera. And then he gave an order he hadn't given in six months. He put the force in his voice that made his crew do what he said. He gave an alpha order to Torren, Nox, Nevada, and Candace. "Come. Here."

Reaching for the camera with his mind, he turned it off. Riyah was staring at the red light that wasn't flashing anymore. Her dark eyes were round with shock. With a small gasp, she blinked and looked at him. Her eyes were still wet with unshed tears, but now they were full of confusion.

"You're not just a mind-reader." She searched his eyes, chest moving fast with her quickening breath. "Witch," she said in a rush.

"I'm not a witch."

She stood quickly and hugged her clipboard to her chest. "I didn't say *you* were."

Holy shit. Vyr sat up straighter. Witch. Riyah was a witch, and that meant she was like him. Other than his mother, he'd never met anyone like him. He'd been alone his whole life with this kind of power, trying to hide it.

There was this moment. The wall lifted in her mind, and she let him in. They were in a dungeon, marked with the scorches of his tortured fire, but all he could see was that trailer from her memories. Inside there were dried plants everywhere, and jars in rows on a table, all labeled. There were stacks of ancient-looking books. The little girl handed the bouquet of flowers to a smiling blond woman with dark, dark freckles all over her face, like Riyah's. "Thank you, my little witch," she murmured, pulling the girl into a hug. It was one of those tight embraces Vyr could feel, even through the memory. He felt hugged. He felt the love between them.

Riyah slammed the door on him again, and as he came back to the room, shocked and touched and hurting and hopeful, two tears streaked down Riyah's cheeks.

"I want your word. Don't burn me."

A witch's biggest fear, right? Death by fire. And she'd come here and risked burning...for his mother? For him? He wanted to know everything, but they were being watched. He could feel eight people in the observation rooms, feel their undivided attention.

He'd never had control over the dragon though, and The Sickening was only making him worse. The meds made him worse. He couldn't make her that promise. He would probably be the death of her if she stuck around. All he could do was explain the monster and hope she would forgive him for the things he would have to do in here.

"You watched the footage of me eating that guard."

She nodded once, and he could smell it—her fear was back. It made him nauseous all over again.

"I can't make you any promises. I'm sorry."

She nodded for a long time, and looked sad. He

was used to that look. He let everyone down. It was best she accepted he wasn't some hero right here and now. It was best she see what he really was—Vyr was fire. He was mindless and deadly when the dragon took him. He was flames that burned up everything he touched.

She gathered the camera and chair and made her way to the door. Something awful snaked in his gut as he realized this was the first and last time he would talk to someone who was anything like him. It would be back to the darkness after this.

"Riyah," he murmured right before she disappeared through the metal exit door.

"Yeah?" she asked in a shaking voice.

"I ate that guard, and I would do it again. I have zero regrets for anyone I've ever devoured. You should know that. But you should also ask yourself why I didn't get any time added to my sentence for eating him."

Her dark eyebrows drew down in confusion. So pretty. He loved her freckles that were like her mom's, and those clear, dark eyes. Windows to a beautiful soul, and he knew it was pure because she'd let him in for a glimpse. He liked the way she smelled like dried plants, and she'd shared a happy memory—something beautiful in the fires of hell. This stranger had given him the best gift he'd ever received. She'd let him feel touch, feel an embrace, feel love right when he'd forgotten what all of that was.

He wanted her to come back. It was selfish. Selfish monster. He would hurt her. He hurt everyone he got close to, but he wanted her to come back and give him pretty moments again.

When she walked out that door, the sound of it clicking closed was the ugliest sound he'd ever heard in his thirty years on this earth.

Then the lights turned off, and he was in the dark once again.

# THREE

*Oh my gosh, oh my gosh, oh my gosh. Settle down, Emmitt's watching. Vyr is like me?*

On a bigger scale though. He was much more powerful than her. She could sense it. He felt like he took up much more space than he actually did because of the power rolling off him in waves. And he'd said he could turn off the volume on the cameras. Had he? Her hands were shaking so bad. Her whole body was. She'd felt him there, in her mind, in that memory when she'd lifted the veil and let him in. When she'd reached out for him. That was a secret memory. One of Mom. One of the happy ones. Before everything went wrong.

*Vyr is like me.*

She'd been alone all these years, hiding, using her powers quietly in her job. She was a counselor because she could calm beastly men and she could sense when they would explode. She could tell who was salvageable.

And that man out there didn't feel salvageable at all. Not even a little bit. He was dark and out of control, and his aura was the color of mud. He was sick—body and head. Barely keeping control. Barely keeping insatiable power at bay. Oh, the guards here didn't have any clue what they were dealing with. If that creature out there...that beautiful, deadly creature...ever got it in his head he wanted to leave, he could blow this prison off the map.

No, he didn't feel salvageable, but Riyah couldn't let him fade to nothing. Couldn't let him fade, couldn't let him use that fire, or it would make everything worse.

He'd called his crew, and now she had to get this video to them somehow. No matter what, this was the most important thing. Every instinct told her she was a part of something big here. She'd always had these feelings. Like when her life took a turn, she could tell if it was important. She could tell if it was a step to something bigger. And she'd been bouncing on stepping stones all her life to get here, to Vyr, to a man who had powers like her.

She wasn't alone.

And she was going to make sure he wasn't alone as he lost his dragon, either. Oh, she knew what "cleansing" did to shifters. She knew the stats. Sixty-four percent of them died from the process. How many had been killed from testing, from IESA, and from the New IESA, and from aaaall the little secret government factions that researched shifters? She couldn't let Vyr be a number. He wasn't salvageable, but he wasn't evil. She knew evil. She could sense it, and that man out there was just trying to keep control of something so, sooooo much bigger than him.

That dragon inside of him…it was a miracle the world was still here at all and not smoke and ashes. Vyr, the human, was hands-down the strongest man she'd ever met. Yet, the media dragged him through the mud.

*Out of control.*
*Put him down.*
*Careless.*

*Man-eater.*

*Unsafe.*

They didn't understand what she now did. Vyr had kept an incredible amount of control over the beast within him. He'd been controlling a monster for three decades, and no one gave him the credit he deserved.

"Emmitt?" she asked casually as she slipped the thumb drive with his interview into her pocket where he couldn't see.

"Hmmm?" he asked, pouring over footage of her interview with Vyr on his monitor. "Fuck, why isn't there any sound on this one either?"

Ha. Because Vyr had way more control of what was happening here than anyone realized.

"Maybe your cameras are malfunctioning?" she wondered in a chaste tone. "Um, how much time did Vyr get added to his sentence for eating that guard?"

"Huh?" Emmitt asked, distracted as he turned up the volume on the speakers to no luck.

"His sentence. How much longer did he get for eating that guard? Number Seventeen."

"Oh. Uh, no extra time."

"Why?" she asked, shuffling her paperwork from

the clipboard into a neat pile.

Emmitt tossed her a dirty look over his shoulder. Instead of answering her question, he said, "At least you got the interview footage. That will surely have volume. I couldn't hear jack shit when you two were talking."

"I think I should do more of these interviews with him. He seemed to open up. It may make him more docile when he needs to be moved, or...fed." Or something. "Why did you turn the lights off on him?" That part pissed her off. From here, she could see his heat signature like snake vision. The man was pure red.

"I told you he's a creature of darkness. We try to keep him calm. His kind like caves, so we do what we can to keep him from going dragon on us."

"But he's human, too. You're keeping a man in the dark with no mental stimulation. That's awful. I want this changed right away."

"Veto."

"I have authority to change his living conditions if they don't meet acceptable standards."

Emmitt sighed loudly, stood, and flipped the switch, turning on the light. "Your ass will be fired as soon as he gets overstimulated and Changes in his cell. He needs to do that in a cage especially made for the dragon. You haven't seen the Change yet, so you aren't careful like you should be..."

Emmitt continued talking, but she tuned him out since she was too busy looking at Vyr, sitting just where she'd left him on the mattress. He wasn't looking at her, but had his chin lowered and was running a hand over and over his shaved head, right over the long scar.

She would bet her tits the New IESA did that, and a part of her didn't even want to know why they'd performed surgery on him. This prison wasn't what it seemed, at least not in the lower levels. This was horrible mistreatment of a prisoner.

"Why no time, Emmitt?" she asked again.

"Because paperwork, Mercer. We all get the big salaries to work down here, but we all signed the same confidentiality and release forms. That's the trade-off. You don't have parents. You don't have family. You don't have friends. You don't have any attachment to the outside world. You know how I know? Because that's one of the requirements to work down here. You have to be completely expendable. Accept that now, and it'll make you careful enough to survive this place. Number Seventeen, Chad, wasn't careful with the monster, and he got himself eaten. No one outside of this facility will be made aware of that fact, and adding to Vyr's sentence would mean paperwork. We have to explain our actions, and that New IESA lab down the hall? They wouldn't let us explain our actions. We would come up missing before that happened."

"You mean people aren't allowed to know what's going on down here because of how you treat the Red Dragon. You don't want the media all over this."

"You sure are a nosy bitch, aren't you?"

"No, I think it's fair to know exactly what I've walked into."

"You're a bad person," Emmitt uttered as he rested his butt against the desk. "Know how I know? Because they wouldn't have hired you if you had morals. And you wouldn't have taken a job like this if you had a conscience. I don't have one either. No one down here does."

"What did Chad do?"

Emmitt shrugged. "Don't know, don't care."

"But Vyr cared enough to eat him."

"Vyr is a monster. He's mindless, and when he gets hungry, he eats. He's not a man. He's pure animal. Wrap your head around that real quick, or you'll be in the belly of the beast next. We have six months and a shit-ton of work to do to make the world safe again. You're part of a super hero squad the world will never know about and will never thank you for. We make the hard decisions to keep it safe from monsters like the Red Dragon. Your only job is to make him steady so we can get him where he needs to be."

"Dragon-less?"

Emmitt smiled, but it never reached his eyes. "No darlin'. Dead."

# FOUR

It was all Riyah could do to get through the rest of the day. She met all the lower-level inmates and eight of the upper levels. Her office was small but worked fine. She was to take on the hardest cases and try to make life in the shifter prison easier for everyone. The aggression in there was off the charts. Twice, she'd watched two silverback gorillas go to war in the cafeteria. No provoking each other either, they just locked eyes across the table and went to blows. And it happened again as the guards were dragging them out. They'd had to tranquilize one of them and Taser the other.

Thankfully, some of the upper-level guards were shifters, so they were strong enough to handle the brutal stuff, but geez, she was feeling way out of her element here.

Her theory? They didn't have shifter guards down on the lower level because they would see what the New IESA and the research lab were doing and cause havoc.

Little did Emmitt fuckin' know, she was the one he needed to worry about, because no matter how long it took and how patient she had to be, she was going to blow the lid right off this place.

Starting with a phone call.

Clara Daye picked up on the second ring. "You're on the burner phone?"

"Yes," Riyah murmured.

"Where are you?"

"Sitting in the parking lot of Fed-Ex. I have something I need to overnight you."

"What is it?"

"Video of your son. It needs to get to his crew, but you should see it first. And Clara?"

"Yeah?"

"I think it's time to bring in Damon."

A deep sigh blasted static on the other end. "Is it that bad?"

"They're killing him."

"What?"

"The New IESA is involved, and they aren't just trying to take his dragon. They want him eliminated, and they can't do it when he's still this strong, so they are killing the dragon first. The second he is weak enough, they are going after Vyr."

"Oh, my God," Clara whispered.

"It gets worse."

"How the fuck can it get worse?" Clara blasted into the phone.

"I toured a research lab on the lower level. They are making something with the tissue and blood samples they've been taking from Vyr."

"Something like what?"

"I don't know. But there was one small room no one was allowed in except the head researcher, and when we passed, it looked like there was a two-person team studying blood and tissue samples. And in the middle of the room was this huge canister that was lit up with a red neon light, and through the window of it, I could see a single vial of something. The room was completely locked down."

"Riyah, did you get a feel for anything in there?"

"Yeah. It was overwhelming, but whatever they're making is huge. There's this underlying current of excitement from the research team. Even when they were meeting me and talking with me, they were still humming with anticipation. Whatever they're making, they're getting close to a breakthrough."

Clara had gone quiet, so Riyah waited a few minutes before she asked, "Are you okay?"

"How is he?"

Riyah shook her head and stared at the Fed-Ex sign, but all she could see was the hollowness in Vyr's eyes and his frozen dragon pupil. "He asked for his crew."

"Shhhhit."

"That's bad?"

"Vyr doesn't need people. He was different growing up. He attached to Torren, so I always knew if he asked for Torren, he was in trouble. But he's asking for his entire crew? He didn't even want to be Alpha."

"What do I do?"

"Ship the video. Ship it to me. I'm bringing Damon in. I should've from the beginning, but I learned a long time ago to let him and Vyr work their own stuff out. Fire versus fire. They're both stubborn men, stubborn dragons. Damon has it in his head that Vyr will do a year in that place, and then his punishment will be done and he'll move on. That's not what's happening, though. Damon trusted a broken system to try and keep things calm between shifters and humans, but it'll get Vyr killed in the process. Time to open my mate's eyes to how bad things really are. We will send the video to the Sons of Beasts."

"And what should I do?"

"Riyah, I need you to keep Vyr steady and keep him strong, remind him of the fight he has in him. I'll get things into motion, but I need time. Be his friend. Be there for him. Be his crew until the Sons of Beasts get there, and when they do, get him as much time with them as possible."

"Six more months in this place won't work. He'll be long dead before he serves the entire sentence."

"Okay." Clara inhaled deeply and repeated, "Okay. If he gets close to the edge before I can line things up…Riyah…get my son out of there. Before they take the dragon, get him out. I can't get anyone else in there to help you, I'm sorry. I tried, and you're all I was able to secure into one of those positions safely.

Help him keep the dragon. Please."

"I'll do the best I can. Clara?"

"Yeah, hon?"

Riyah dipped her voice to a whisper. "He's like me."

"I know. Damon and I have watched you for a long time, Riyah. We knew of your parents. I'm sorry for everything that happened. I know it's lonely. I was like that, too, until I found Damon. Vyr struggles with feeling alone as well. You have always felt important, but I couldn't figure out why. And now I keep getting this feeling that you're supposed to be there with him."

A strange sense of déjà vu took her. She'd been thinking the same thing lately. Like the stars were lining up, and her journey could be epic or end in disaster.

She just didn't know which one yet.

# FIVE

Riyah plopped onto the couch and rested the carton of chocolate chip cookie dough ice cream on her stomach before she flipped channels, looking for something good to watch. The small apartment was full of boxes she would never unpack because this would never be home. She had a wandering problem. A year at her last job was the longest she'd ever stayed in one place since her parents passed. A few months in, and she would get restless and continue the search for the elusive "home" she'd always craved but never found.

She changed channels until she tracked down a show about Alaska homesteaders and pulled the blanket over her lap, then scooped a spoon of ice cream.

*"You're still awake."*

Riyah jumped so hard she dropped the spoon onto the laminate flooring with a clatter. Terrified, she looked around, but she was alone. "H-hello?"

*"Don't be scared. I can't burn you from here, Witch."*

"V-Vyr?" she whispered. Fuck! She squeezed her eyes tightly shut and focused, slamming her mind closed.

There. She couldn't feel him anymore.

Panting, she sat there too scared to move. He'd sounded as if he was sitting right beside her when he spoke. What the hell? He could reach into her mind all the way from the lower levels of the prison? The amount of power he possessed to be able to do such a thing was horrifying. It had built an instant headache behind her eyes. Even with him far away, he could hurt her.

But...

This was kind of like a phone call...right?

Vyr could talk to her. Could she talk back, like when they were facing each other in the prison?

Slowly, she relaxed and opened her mind again.

He was gone. She couldn't feel him anywhere, and the headache had faded as though it had never existed. She tried reaching out for him, but there was nothing to hold onto, and she got mentally exhausted within moments. She would need to use some of Mom's spells to make her stronger if she wanted to do this. Already she was ticking off a list of plants, herbs, and powders she would need. The spell books were in a box in the corner. She hadn't looked at them in years, but maybe it was time to dust them off.

She couldn't focus on the show anymore. She tried for half an hour, but she kept thinking about Vyr and part of her wished he would come back. She'd reacted out of fear, closing her mind like that, and maybe it had pushed him away forever. She should be relieved, but instead, she felt hollow.

Giving up on relaxing before bed, she got up and brushed her teeth and washed her face. It was still early to sleep, but maybe she could get her body to wind down. The alarm would come early enough in the morning.

But as she lay in bed, she thought about Vyr's eyes, his harsh smile, and straight, white teeth. She tried to remember the footage of his dragon eating that guard, but she kept drifting back to the way his arms pushed against the thin material of his white T-shirt, the way his tattoo ink trailed down his arm to his inner elbow. Even on death's door, he was a gorgeous man.

*"Thank you."*

She'd been half asleep, but Riyah jerked up in bed. "You're back."

A deep chuckle echoed through her head. *"I tried to leave you alone like you wanted. It's boring as fuck in here though, so I figured I would try again. What are you doing?"*

"I'm lying in bed. And I feel like a crazy person for talking out loud to myself."

*"Maybe you are crazy. Maybe I'm not really in your head. Maybe you just want to talk to me so badly that you're making all of this up."*

"Are the lights off?" she asked.

There was a mental shrug. *"They turned them back off right after you left. I got punished. They made me eat dinner in the dark, too. They have the flashing lights of the hangar doors going though, so there's that. I'll probably go insane and twitchy by the next time you see me. Prep yourself. You might not think I look so hot tomorrow."*

"I didn't say hot."

*"Were you going to touch yourself to me?"*

"Stop, or I'll kick you out again and let you rot in the dark."

*"If I could, I would be jacking off to you. But there are eight grown dudes in the observation rooms. Turns me off."*

Riyah bit back a smile. "You would really jack off to me?"

*"Hell, yeah. You're hot, too."*

"Is this what mental conversations will be like with you? All perverted stuff? Don't tell me you're one of those guys."

*"I'm absolutely one of those guys, but okay. Let us pretend to not be attracted to one another. What would you like to talk about?"*

Riyah smiled even bigger. "Sometimes you say things strangely."

*"What do you mean?"*

"You say them all formal."

*"It's how my dad talks. Momma bear curses like a sailor, Daddy dragon is millennia old, an ancient who only turned mortal when he met my mom, so he grew*

*up in a different time where manners were everything. Blame him for turning me into this."*

Vyr's voice had gone all dark though, and had lost the edge of humor he had earlier.

"You mean blame him for the dragon part?"

*"Blame him for everything if you want. You're a counselor, right? Prison psychologist? You'll love me. Daddy issues for days. What are you doing? Paint me a picture."*

She giggled and relaxed back in bed. "I'm under mismatched sheets, in my twin-sized bed, in my apartment that is full of boxes from moving. I'm too lazy to unpack them, and I'm fine with clutter."

*"Strike one. I hate clutter."*

"I'm wearing pajama pants with cartoon tacos on them and a white tank top."

*"Bra or no bra?"*

"Sports bra."

*"Strike two. What color panties?"*

"Get ready for a supermassive boner."

*"I'm prepared."*

"Beige."

*"And there's your strike three. You're a boner killer."*

"You're welcome. Now you don't have to worry about those eight dudes watching you adjust yourself."

Another chuckle sounded, low and soft, and it made her smile on reflex. "You have a nice laugh."

*"I can't sleep lately."* He said it suddenly as though he wanted to do it before he could change his mind.

"Why not?"

*"I think it's the meds. Or The Sickening."*

"What is The Sickening?"

*"I've been away from my crew and my mountains too long. It started out as nosebleeds, but now I hear things and see things that aren't there. I feel sick even when I don't have the meds in my body. Sometimes I Change without knowing. I just...come to and I've burned the room again."*

"What did that guard do? The one you ate?"

*"He hurt little girls. Thought about it all the time. He was remorseless, and his memories were so loud I couldn't help but see what he did. Emmitt talks about the lower level being hell, and I'm the devil himself, right? Maybe. But I'm not the only one down here. Paperwork means they'll have to admit what caliber of guards they hire down here. And they would have to do*

*it publicly. Subject change. Why peonies? In your memory, you had a bouquet of them."*

Riyah swallowed bile at his admission about the man he'd eaten. How awful. She struggled to catch up with the new conversation and stuttered when she said, "Th-they were my mom's favorite."

*"My mom likes wildflowers. My dad used to buy her big bouquets of expensive roses, but she was never as impressed as when he would go into the yard and pick her some little pink wildflowers. She would put them in this little shot glass and keep them alive for two weeks."*

"That sounds romantic."

*"Oh yeah, my parents would make you puke with their cuteness. Most people don't get to see it because my dad is so reserved. He has to look in control all the time. But in my house, growing up, I watched them. I used to think I wanted that someday, too."*

"You don't anymore?"

*"Nope. I want dirty talk and beige panties. Wear some extra hideous ones tomorrow, and I'll guess the color."*

"Deal," she said with a laugh. "I'll call them Vyr-panties."

A satisfied, sexy rumble vibrated through her mind. *"Good girl."*

Holy hell, he was sexy.

*"Thank you."*

"Stop that."

*"I think you are sexy, too. I like your freckles."*

Riyah pressed her fingertips against her heated cheek. "Really?"

*"Do you have freckles on your shoulders?"*

"Yes."

*"Back?"*

"Yes, and a birthmark. A tiny one under my right shoulder blade."

*"Mmmm. Who knows about that?"*

"Just you. I don't think anyone has paid attention to it before. Why is it so easy to talk to you?"

*"Because you're crazy, and you're really only talking to yourself."*

"Jerk."

He chuckled again. God, she liked when he did that.

*"These damn flashing lights are going to drive me insane."*

"Put your pillow over your face."

*"Trying to suffocate me already?"*

"No, to block out the light. I'll talk to them about the flashing lights tomorrow and leaving you in the damn dark. It makes me want to stab Emmitt for doing this. Do you want me to tell you boring stories until you get tired? I'm pretty good at them."

*"Back up, woman. Did you just get protective?"*

"Maybe." She smiled at the slowly turning ceiling fan she could barely see in the dark. "It's bullshit is all I'm saying. If they're gonna kill you, they might as well try and make it comfortable."

*"Right? I've been trying to tell them that all along. They gave me actual gruel for dinner. Makes me wish they would speed the process along, but maybe that's the point."*

She giggled. "We should not be joking about this. It's horrible of us, and not funny at all."

*"You're right. Let's cry together instead. That solves all problems."*

She rolled her eyes and sighed. "I suppose joking is better. Just so you know, I'm not going to let them kill you, though."

*"Oh, are you my knight-ess in shining stilettos?"*

"Yep. I'm the heroine to your story. Don't eat me

before I get my job done."

*"Hmm. Eat you, eat you?"* His voice dipped lower and went sultry. *"Or eat you?"*

"Perv."

*"I'll wait right here while you touch yourself."*

"Okay, I'm going to sleep now."

*"You can't. You already told me you would tell me boring stories, and you should never break a promise to a dying man. That's seven years bad luck."*

"I think that's if you break a mirror."

*"Potato Potah-toh. God, I would literally kill for potatoes. Six months on lower level food, and I'm bored out of my mind. And beer. I would do awful things for a beer."*

"Hey, beer rhymes with Vyr."

*"Ha. One of my crew calls me 'Beer' sometimes just to piss me off."* Vyr got quiet for a few seconds. *"I would also kill to hear Nox call me Beer again. I miss their stupid voices."*

"Do you like being alpha?"

*"No. I suck at it. I don't care enough about keeping the crew quiet to keep us safe. And now look what I've done? I called my crew to me. Asked them to put themselves in this awful place just to try and prolong*

*my life. Alphas are supposed to be selfless, and I'm not. I'm a selfish creature."*

"Because you want to live. It's not selfish."

*"Mmm. A good alpha would put his crew before himself. But mostly they put themselves before me. They tried to keep me steady, keep me from destroying things. Subject change. What did you eat for dinner? I'm serious when I say the food is boring here and I want to live vicariously through you."*

"A TV dinner. Chicken nuggets and squishy macaroni and cheese and little asparagus bites."

*"Ew. Strike four."*

She snorted. "Judgmental. I don't have my kitchen unpacked yet."

*"If I was out of here, I would help you unpack."*

It was so unexpectedly sweet of him to say, she didn't know how to respond. Her stomach dipped with butterflies, and she pursed her lips against a mushy smile. "Admission—I'm not good at unpacking because I never stay in one place long enough, so what's the point?"

*"A roamer?"*

"I guess. I'm restless in general. Are you going to say strike five?"

*"Nope. I wish I could be a roamer right now. Pacing this damn cell isn't all it's cracked up to be."*

"What are you doing now?"

*"Pulling the pillow off my face, giving up on sleep, and I'm going to do pushups until my arms won't hold me up anymore. Your bedtime stories weren't boring enough."*

"I'll try harder then. Tell me every ten pushups so I can cheer you on, though."

*"Ten."*

"Already?"

*"Twenty."*

"Good, lord. Okay, tell me every hundred pushups or I'll never get through a bedtime story. Once upon a time…"

Vyr huffed a laugh.

"There was this badass who Tasered Emmitt for fucking calling her a princess, and there was this hornball dragon who—"

*"No, I want a real story. One about your life. One hundred."*

"Go, Vyr, go. Do all the pushups." She wracked her brain for a memory. "Okaaay, let me see. We used to have peach trees."

*"Oh, good, this sounds super boring. I think I'm getting tired already."*

"Not polite. We had this orchard behind the trailer I grew up in. I loved it out there. My dad was normal. Human with no powers, and he worked a lot so my mom didn't have to. She couldn't."

*"Why not?"*

"Because she had powers like us, but she couldn't control them very well. She had anxiety around strangers and would lose control. Shifters were just coming out to the public, and we were watching all the fights and protests on the news every night. My parents were scared of someone finding out about my mom. There aren't many natural-born witches, so we were very careful. We didn't have much, my dad was a miner, but we had enough. But when the peaches grew, my mom would always get brave and sell them at a farmer's market. She would prep herself for weeks to be around people, collecting herbs that would stunt her powers, casting spells that would keep her steady. Keep her numb to all that extra energy of the market maybe, I don't know. But we would work so hard, my mom and I, picking these peaches and loading them into crates, and we would drive our old dodge pickup to the farmer's market and sell those peaches. They were the best. I still remember exactly what they tasted like. Sometimes my mom and I would get hungry and tired of picking, so we would sit down and just...pig out. They were the juicy kind too, so we would be covered in sticky-sweet peach juice. Bees were always buzzing around us. The last few years, my mom would make peach preserves, and we sold those, too. Farmer's market months, we would get to go buck wild at the grocery store because we had extra money. My mom would let me get Jell-O, candy, Fruit Roll-ups, and the expensive cereal.

*"What happened to her?"*

An explosion flashed in her mind. Her outstretched fingers, sobbing...the predators. The animals. The pain of the power she hadn't been able to control. She flinched away from the memory. "Subject change."

A soft, prehistoric growl filled her head. *"Two hundred."*

"Tired yet?"

*"No. If I don't make it out of here—"*

"Don't say that."

*"No listen. If I don't, I need you to do something for me. I know it's rude for me to ask you something when we don't know each other, but I don't have a connection to anyone else outside of here. I can't reach my crew. I've tried. For some reason, you're the only one I can communicate with on the outside."*

"Okay." She swallowed hard and curled on her side in a ball. "Ask."

*"If something happens and I lose this battle...tell my people I went strong, okay? Tell them I didn't let the New IESA and the prison break me, even if you see it differently...fuck."*

"What's wrong?"

*"Nosebleed. Hang on, I'll be right back. Don't go to sleep yet. I want to say goodnight. I'll hurry."*

"Hurry and do what?"

*"It's too much blood. I'm trying to get a guard's attention. Everything is okay."*

And then there was deafening silence.

"Vyr?" Riyah sat up in bed. "Vyr, are you there? Are you okay?"

By the time ten minutes had passed, Riyah was up and pacing the room. "Vyr, are you there?" Shit. She pulled on a pair of jeans, high heels, and a nice black blouse. Grabbed her bag and jogged as best she could in her work shoes to her Xterra. Shit, shit, shit, Vyr was bleeding. It had been too long since he Changed, since he'd been around his crew and his mountains. He was being dragged to his knees, and she couldn't just lay in bed when he was going through another wave of The Sickening.

Wait. She sat in her car, gripping the wheel, panting. Riyah needed to think clearly before she acted. She had access to the prison whenever she wanted. She was on call at all times in case one of the inmates needed her services. But if she ran in there, guns blazing at the same exact time Vyr was bleeding, it would throw suspicion on them both. If the New IESA didn't know he could read minds, she had to protect him from them finding out. "Vyr, please. Just tell me you're okay. Tell me now or I'm coming to you."

Another minute passed. She muttered a curse and turned on the SUV.

*"Stop. Riyah, it's late. Turn off the car. I'm okay."*
"Where are you?"
*"I'm sitting in my cell, on the bed, leaned against the wall. There is a hazmat team cleaning up the mess.*

*Everything is okay. I'm calm."*

"Is your fist clenched?"

*"What?"*

"Is your fist clenched?"

There were a few seconds of hesitation and then, *"Yes."*

He wasn't okay then. Not really. "Someday I want a peach orchard of my own. I want peach trees. I want to pick the fruit and sell it at a farmer's market because those are some of my favorite times."

*"What happened to her, Riyah?"*

"I can't tell you now because it won't help you. But in a week, when you're still here, still fighting, still being your badass self, I'll tell you all about it."

*"I have a pet swan."*

Riyah heaved a sigh and got out of her car, shut the door behind her, and locked it. "I'll have you know I just put on high heels in the middle of the night to come save you from a nosebleed. I think we are friends now. What is your swan's name?"

Vyr made an annoyed ticking sound. *"It was supposed to be Fergus, but Nox renamed him Mr. Diddles. I have this goddamn majestic swan named Mr. Diddles now, and I used to hate it, but lately I call him that in my head. I wonder if he's still alive or if Nox has eaten him yet. I found him when he was this ugly, little baby. He was alone at this park I used to go to clear my head. The parents were gone, and he was this hideous, little, gray, fuzzy thing with a messed-up wing. A cat got him or something. I did what I could but his wing was messed up forever. He would never fly, and I was gutted for him. How sad that he would never hit an air current. And yeah, I know they aren't great flyers, but still."*

"You felt for him."

"Yeah."

"Because you don't let yourself feel the sky very much."

*"I can't. If I Changed as much as I want, the world would be ash."*

"So you gave up the sky."

*"So I stay on the ground where I'm most uncomfortable, just like Mr. Diddles. Are you back in your apartment safe?"*

"Yes, just got back into my bedroom. Getting back into my PJs."

*"Veto, just wear those sexy brown panties tonight. Feel those sheets on your skin."*

"Perv."

*"Not this time. I sleep in just underwear. At least I did before this place. The feel of sheets on my back is good. I used to wake up just to think, 'Damn, that feels nice,' before I fell asleep again. Sleep in your panties for me because I can't."*

Riyah hesitated, then pushed her PJ pants back down her legs and crawled into bed in just her panties. "Is the hazmat team still there?"

*"Just finishing up. I'm trying to stay out of their heads. Monsters, monsters, all around."*

"Is your fist still clenched."

*"...yes."*

"Tell me what you miss the most."

*"What do I miss the most? The sky. The stars. Sometimes I like to think that even if I can't see them, they're smiling down on me. And sure, the smiles are sad because they miss me too, and can see I'm going through hell. They hurt for me...but their smiles exist because they can also see something better coming."*

Wow. Riyah held a pillow close and stared at the dark doorframe of the on-suite bathroom. Vyr was deep. He was real. He wasn't monster. Everyone was so, sooo wrong about him.

*"That means a lot."*

"Huh?"

*"You said people are wrong about me. You don't think I'm a monster. You're one of the first people to think that."*

"I forget you're in my head sometimes. Feels like you are right here, lying beside me in the dark instead of miles away underground."

*"Will you miss me when I'm gone?"*

"No."

*"Pity."*

"Because you aren't going anywhere." Riyah yawned and snuggled her face against the pillow.

*"The badass princess and the broken dragon*, Vyr said softly. *Emmitt doesn't know you're a queen, and perhaps you shouldn't let him know you are boss down here. Maybe let him think he is the power for a while. Watch what happens down here. Wait. The New IESA is making a weapon. I can see their thoughts. I can see how close they are getting. Someday, when I'm too weak to fix it, you may have to use those powers of yours and step in. Save the world and shit."*

"What are they making?"

*"They're making a new dragon. I can't Turn a new*

*dragon, and they're working out a way to change that."*

"Only certain shifters can Change their mates, right?"

*"Correct. The New IESA is killing my dragon, but they are putting part of him in a bottle, and they are going to save it for when they want a red dragon they can control."*

"Oh, my God." Out of all the scenarios she'd been considered down in that mad scientist lab, creating a dragon serum hadn't even crossed her mind. "That could change everything."

*"It will wreck the world. All they have to do is put my dragon in someone who isn't strong enough, and that power can be unleashed on everything. They think they can make the dragon less aggressive with gene therapy. They're wrong. So wrong. Dragons aren't creatures you tame. They're creatures you try not to piss off. The second they try to control the dragon they make? He'll be the new Apocalypse. The new End of Days."*

"Jesus."

*"Jesus has nothing to do with what they are doing in that lab. You yawned earlier. Are you tired?"*

"A little. I have to be up early to go to work."

*"To see me."*

Riyah giggled. "Yes, I have an early morning therapy session scheduled with this really crazy dragon shifter I met today. He's kinda cute, but he's an easy bleeder."

Vyr snorted. *"Hey...don't look at the video from tonight, okay? I don't want you seeing me like that."*

"I need to see everything."

*"You don't. For me, just...don't. I'll see you in the morning, Riyah. Enjoy those sheets on your skin. Wish I was there."*

"Perv."

*"Nah, I would let you sleep. Would be a complete gentlemen and sleep on the couch. But I would keep the nightmares away. I can do that, you know."*

"I think you can do a lot of things people don't realize. How do you know about the nightmares?"

*"I saw what happened to your mom. I didn't mean to. It was there, a bright memory when you were talking about the peaches. Someday you're going to get your orchard. Goodnight, Badass Princess."*

Riyah hugged the pillow against her stomach. "I'll see you in the morning. Goodnight, Broken Dragon."

*"Hey, Riyah?"*

"Yeah, Vyr?

*"Thanks for helping me unclench my fist."*

She smiled to herself in the dark. "Anytime."

# SIX

The video didn't make sense.

All she could do was stare at the man in the grainy footage, on his hands and knees and coughing rivers of blood, every muscle flexed, a look of agony written on his face until he finally fell over on his side, crimson streaming from his mouth and nose as he stared blankly at the video camera. He'd been talking to her in his head while he'd been going through this.

"I need help," he said out loud, his body convulsing. "Guards," he said a little louder. "Help."

Rage racked her body at how long it took for the hangar doors to open. Two of the frontrunner guards shot him with darts in the back as he lay there, not fighting. Three more guards lifted him into a seated position on the bed, and one threw a white towel at his face. It fell in his lap, but Vyr didn't move to clean himself up. He wasn't done bleeding yet.

Riyah stared at that clenched fist of his, resting on his knee, his hand shaking so bad as a crew cleaned the blood on the floor.

And what had he done? He'd reassured her so she could stay home safe and go to sleep. He was in agony, and yet he'd talked to her like everything was okay.

Vyr was the strongest man she'd ever met.

But the witch inside of her burned to crush the guards down here. She couldn't even breathe for the red rage inside of her.

A squeaking noise sounded as Emmitt kicked the toe of his shoe against the tile floor. "They call it The Sickening. We had to force it a bit because Vyr wasn't showing signs yet. He's old enough that he should have started it already. He never settled with a mate, and they tend to start getting sick if they don't find a treasure in their late twenties. This one's different, though. He's the son of Damon Daye, and he's an original. An ancient. Vyr is stronger. A different breed perhaps. So...we took him from his mountains, and we gave him meds to kickstart The Sickening.

"You don't have a problem with any of this?" she asked, straitening up and looking Emmitt dead in the eyes.

"Nope. I've seen the video of him burning Covington. I have no problem saving the world. I'm a goddamn hero."

Riyah shook her head slowly and gave him a ghost of a smile. Someday, she was going to get revenge for Vyr. And she was going to start with Emmitt, the pretend hero.

"How long has it been since he Changed?"

"Since number seventeen. Three weeks ago. He's about due again, but it's a big production. You're here, though." Emmitt matched her empty smile. "That's part of your job, Princess. Make the Changes manageable when they have to happen. Keep him in control with your psychotherapy mumbo-jumbo bullshit like everyone seems to think you can do. We just need him to Change and sit quietly in his cage like a good little pet dragon until he can Change back into a human again. So far, there's been too much fire when a Change goes down."

"Why don't you just kill him and get it over with?"

"Can't. We've tried. Each time we try, the Red Dragon comes out and people get hurt. We need him weaker. Weaken him, Mercer. That's why they're paying you the big bucks."

She wanted to puke. Right here in Emmitt's observation room, she wanted to vomit.

The door opened, and a tank of a man with dark hair, a dark beard, and icy blue eyes leaned in. He had on the same guard uniform as Emmitt. He jerked his chin at the head guard. "Hey boss, they're pulling us in for a meeting."

Emmitt sighed. "Riyah Mercer, this is Hank Butte, and he is on the lower level team. He helps me run security down here. He came in six months ago with the Red Dragon. He was responsible for bringing the monster in."

Hank Butte was a shifter. She could tell from the churning, inhuman blue of his eyes and from the awful feeling in her gut she got when he looked at her. He was very dominant, very powerful, and a bad man with loyalty to no one. There was a chip missing with him. She couldn't sense any empathy from him at all. He was just a shadow. Empty. No feelings. Dark.

But then, he would have to be if he was a shifter and could watch what was happening to his people down here. This douche-nugget brought Vyr in? Oh good, now she was justified in instantly hating him.

"Pleasure to meet you," she said, not even trying to sound sincere.

"Yeah, I don't give a fuck about meeting you either, lady. They want us in that meeting in ten—" He returned his attention to Vyr. "Oh, shit!" The towering man startled and his eyes went wide as he looked at the window behind her.

When Riyah turned around, Vyr was standing right up against the window, a feral smile on his face, eyes locked on Butte. He looked like a damn demon, his eyes both silver with that elongated pupil.

"I don't think he likes you," Riyah murmured, crossing her arms.

Vyr's smile widened, his predatory gaze still on Butte.

"Better hope he never does a jailbreak, boys. I don't think you two would be safe from his fire."

"Fuckin' creepy dragon," Emmitt muttered, shoving Butte out the door. Before he left, he turned back around and jammed a finger at her. "If you go in there, you make sure there are six in the observation rooms and a team on standby to get you out of there if you need help."

"You care," she said with a too bright smile.

"Nope. I just hate when this place stinks like burning human flesh. Makes it hard to eat lunch down here for a week. Don't die, Princess."

After the metal door swung closed behind him, she flipped him off. When she turned around, Vyr was still there. He was looking at her with a sexyboy smirk. His eyes were still both silver, but he lifted a hand slowly and pressed it against the glass, locked his arm like he was just leaning against a wall.

Before she could change her mind and chicken out, she approached the window and pressed her palm against the glass, too. His palm was so much bigger than hers.

*"Don't get caught alone with Butte. If you ever do, call me. Call the dragon. If I'm still strong enough, I'll fix it."*

Just in case the room was bugged, she didn't speak. Instead, she nodded and hoped he would sense it. She shouldn't feel safe with Vyr, but she did. And right now? She didn't really care what that said about her. She believed him. He would burn this place to the ground to protect her. It made no sense to trust a man like this. To trust the baddest shifter on Earth, locked in the lower levels of a high-security prison. But as she watched him straighten his spine and his hand slip from the smooth surface...as she watched him make his way to the bed, she knew she trusted Vyr a hundred times more than she trusted the "hero" guards here. The wrong bad guy was locked up.

She used the intercom that was connected to the other observation rooms and checked them one at a time, made sure there were six in there and an extraction team. She would mind Emmitt's rules. For now.

And then she used her card to get through the two steel doors into Vyr's cell. He lifted his smoldering gaze and tracked her progress across the cavernous room. Formally, he gestured to a plastic chair in front of the bed. *"You look sexy as fuck,"* his voice rumbled in her head. Out loud he asked innocently, "Back for more interviews?" A slow smile stretched his face as he dipped into her mind again and murmured, *"Blue. You're wearing blue Vyr-*

*panties. Right?"*

"I told you yesterday I wasn't good at these, but I guess this is my life now. At least you don't suck at interviews too bad." She hid a smile. "You're making me blush *red*."

*"Red Vyr-panties. Fuuuuuck. Red for my dragon, right? Say yes."*

"And *yes* to more interviews. It's part of my job, to study what you're going through and help you through this transition."

Vyr's smile turned hungry, and when a deep rumble shook the room, she sat in the chair in a hurry so she didn't lose her balance.

"The dragon wants out. It's been too long. I won't have control much longer. If you're taking requests on what will make this easier? I need to Change."

Riyah wrote that down word for word on the lined paper she'd attached to her clipboard. "Anything else?"

*"Conjugal visits. Watch that wicked smile, woman, we are being monitored."*

Riyah wiped her face clean of a smile and cleared her throat as she looked at him again. "How are you feeling today?"

"Like shit. I had a rough night. I think you know that, though. How did you like that footage?" Something hard flashed through his silver eyes.

"I did watch it—"

*"I asked you not to."*

"—because I need to see what living in here is really like for you."

*"You're going to watch me break, Badass Princess."*

"I need to ensure you make it to the end of your sentence, and that means being involved in every stage of your transition here."

*"Riyah—"*

"It doesn't make you weak," she said, cutting off his thoughts rattling around in her head. "But I need to see everything. For me. It helps."

*"Helps how? Seriously, how could watching me damn near bleed out every night help you?"*

"You are a very powerful creature, Vyr Daye."

*"So?"*

She glared at him. "Me, too."

The cameras in the upper corners popped and sparked, and the lights went out. She was immersed in total darkness, and she could hear the guards yelling outside the hangar doors, as if they couldn't open them. What the fuck?

"We have thirty seconds. What do you mean?" Vyr asked in the dark.

"Watching you suffer feeds my power. I fucking told you I'm not letting you die. If I have to step in, I need to be at the top of my game. Fuel me with your suffering, Red Dragon."

A hand gripped her forearm in the dark, and she was yanked forward. And then his lips crashed onto hers. There was a powerful, vibrating rumble that rattled straight through her, but she didn't care. Desperate for the last few seconds with him, she parted her lips and let him thrust his tongue inside her mouth. He slid his hand up her bare leg and under the hem of her dress to her panties. He made it to her upper thigh and gripped her so hard she gasped at the pleasure and pain. His fingers dug into her skin as he kissed her. Chaos reigned with the sounds of yelling and panic outside the hangar doors, but for this moment, it was just her and Vyr.

He bit her bottom lip hard and released her suddenly. "Compose yourself. You've got five seconds."

Breath hitching, she straightened her dress and

licked her bottom lip in case it was bleeding. She didn't taste iron, though. She stood and picked up the chair, and when the lights came on, she was poised like a lion-tamer, keeping a big-cat away. Vyr sat on the bed, relaxed, hands unclenched as he watched her jab the chair legs at him.

"What just happened?" she screamed as the hangar doors blasted upward and a team of four wearing fireproof gear came slinking in, rifles trained on Vyr. "Who did that?"

"Technical glitch, ma'am," one of the guards murmured as he grabbed her around the waist and dragged her back toward the open hangar door. "You're okay. Everything's okay. We've got you."

And in the second just before the hangar door slammed closed, Vyr gifted her with a wicked smile.

# SEVEN

"Well, what can we do to reduce the anger?" Riyah asked in her calmest voice as the giant grizzly shifter with the blazing white eyes glared at her from across her desk.

"Ain't no quick fix, Doc. You can kill me, that's about it." He stood so quickly the chair behind him blasted backward and smashed into the wall, making yet another hole in the sheetrock. Great. "It was really fuckin' nice to talk to you and get nothing accomplished but hey, at least I missed my shift at the commissary, and now I'm down another dollar of wage, so thanks a bunch for abso-fuckin-lutely nothin'."

"Well maybe you should stop making shanks and

plotting to kill your cellmate, Daniel," she said cheerfully. "See you tomorrow."

Daniel spat on the cement floor and flipped her off. Only his hands were in handcuffs behind his back, so she had to purse her lips against a smile at him struggling with his middle finger. Sometimes the inmates were awesome and wanted to improve their situation, and sometimes they were Daniels.

Two guards led him out of her office, and the door clicked closed behind him. She did her best not to jump out of her skin when he slammed his forehead against her front window and stared at her for three terrifying seconds before the guards shoved him down the hallway. Today had been a pill. And she missed Vyr. When she had these appointments, she shut him out so he didn't get riled up. He didn't like that she was in this room with the baddies of the prison. Didn't like that he couldn't help if she got in trouble. And sure, she was completely capable of handling herself in these situations since her training had prepared her for this job, but it was really nice having someone care if she was okay.

She pressed her finger on the screen of her tablet, waited for it to read her fingerprint, then entered in ilikebigdicksandicannotlie69 and then she said her name to get through all the security. When it opened up on her notes, she skipped to Vyr's and began to read.

*~~Subject~~ Inmate: Vyr Daye*

*June 7 – First day of observation – Standoffish, defensive, very powerful, struggling for control, sick, defeated, quiet, angry, dragon is half-dead. Huge changes need to be made for him if he is to survive this another six months.*

*June 8 – Second day of observation – Last night was eventful. He was in my head. It was nerve-wracking at first, but then I was comfortable with him there very quickly. He controls a great deal of power, and no one knows what it's like for him. This is a man who has been misunderstood his entire life, from the second he was born, and still, he hasn't quit on humans. He didn't stop trying to protect people from himself, even when they ripped him apart in the media. Flawed, deep-rooted anger stemming from childhood, showing a great devotion to very few, loyal, protective. Cute. He had a nosebleed though, and it opened my eyes to how bad things get for him locked down there. Things need to turn around immediately. I'm asking Emmitt to keep the lights on and give me 24/7 video access to Vyr. I'm also asking for an improvement to his diet and some sheets for his bed.*

*June 9 – Third day of observation. I can't stop thinking about when the lights went off. The way his hand felt up my skirt. The way his lips felt against mine. The rasp of three-day stubble against my cheek. The way he tasted faintly of mint and smoke. The sound of his dragon growling and the hungry look in his eyes when the guards took me away from him. The way he immediately asked in my head if I was okay when I left his line of sight. The way I have five perfect fingerprint bruises on my thigh, and I think he did it on purpose just so I would think about him later. I should be terrified of that man, and not just because he could burn me, but because he feels like trouble. To my heart. And I can't conjure up the fear I know I should feel because all I keep thinking about is how rough his hand was, but how soft his kiss turned at the end. I'm in trouble.*

*June 10 – Stayed up all night talking to a cute boy with red hair, and now I'm exhausted. Vyr is really, really different from what I thought he would be. I'm three coffees in. I just went into the cell, which Emmitt is now calling "The Lair," but Vyr popped off that this hellhole wasn't his lair. When Emmitt asked him what he meant, Vyr smiled like a demon and told him he should visit his mountains sometime. That his crew would probably welcome him right in. I had this vision of a silverback and a grizzly ripping Emmitt limb from limb, and I'm pretty sure that was Vyr's imagination in my head. That was new. He projected into me. Am I getting more powerful? Or is he?*

*It's after lunch, and they aren't feeding him right. Every time I complain, Emmitt points out that Vyr has somehow put on ten pounds of muscle since he's been locked down there, which kind of blows my mind. The dragon gets weaker, and the man gets stronger. At least that's what it looks like to the casual observer. Vyr had another nosebleed right before I left. It started as a trickle down his lip, and I pointed it out. I handed him a rag from his bathroom station, but a minute in, and the rag was soaked through. He asked me to leave, and I wanted to cry because I knew how it was going to be for him. I saw how it was on that video, and I don't want him alone with the guards. They're too rough when he's weak like that. Vyr asked the guards to take me away when I refused to go, and they did. And now I'm sitting here looking at this ham sandwich, wishing I was eating in Vyr's cell with him, splitting my lunch, giving him half my sandwich and half my chips and half my orange Fanta. And a potato. I wish I could give him a potato. He's been hungry for starches lately. Craving them, and I think there is some serious nutrition missing from his diet. I think Emmitt is trying to weaken him with malnutrition, but it's not working. Tomorrow they are going to let him Change. I say "let him" but it's really "force him" to Change. They like him to Change in a controlled setting, if anyone can really control the Red Dragon. Everyone is bustling around preparing for the Change in some place they call 'The Dungeon,' and meanwhile I annoyed Emmitt enough to do a surprise for Vyr when he's done.*

*Sometimes I want to tell Vyr to burn this place to the ground.*

*I shouldn't write that, shouldn't even think it, but it's there in the back of my mind. This constant, buzzing wish that grows bigger every time I see him mistreated. I wish he could escape and hide forever, but where on this planet can the Red Dragon stay a secret? He's too big and too destructive. I can see why his father wanted him in here. I'm pissed that he helped, but I understand Vyr has to serve this sentence if he wants to have a shot at living a life where he isn't on the run.*

*Clara just texted the burner phone. I don't understand what "Incoming" means, but it feels big. And yep, I'm now writing my notes on my tablet because, apparently, I can't stay professional with Vyr, and I need a secure way to write down my thoughts on all of this. His notes have gone from professional observations to what looks like my middle-school-self's Hello Kitty diary when I had a crush on Gus Naydor.*

*"Who's Gus Naydor and where does he live?"* Vyr asked in her head. His voice was a little too careful.

With a grin, Riyah checked that the hallway outside of her office was clear, leaned back in her rolling chair, and flicked her fingers. The blinds closed instantly, and on her desk, a pen stood upright and began scribbling a heart onto a yellow notepad. "Jealous?" she asked in a low murmur so no one walking by outside the office would hear her. Shifters had impeccable hearing though, so she set the phone right beside her just in case she needed to fake talking on it if anyone barged in.

*"I told you, I don't feel. Jealousy is a feeling, therefore no. I don't want to burn Gus Naydor and devour his ashes."*

She snorted and shook her head. "Beast."

*"I wish I could take you out."*

The admission was sudden, and Riyah sat up straighter in her chair. "I haven't been on a date in over a year. What if I'm a total bore, and you don't like me anymore?"

*"I would give a helluva lot to have you bore me over dinner. We both know I'm not getting out of here, though. Forget it. I was just talking."*

She moved the pen's rhythm to make a crack down the center of the heart. "If you do get out, will you ask me out sweetly?"

*"What, like writing it across the sky? Hot air balloons and signs?"*

"No, not something expensive. I don't care about that stuff. Just ask me sweet."

There was a mental sigh and then, *"Well, it's good that money isn't your love language because this dragon is broke as hell. The government froze my accounts when I burned Covington, and now they've drained them all for damages to the town. I was a rich boy, and now I'm a—"*

"Regular guy. Lucky you."

*"Regular guy. Who turns into a dragon. Who watches guards run themselves ragged to plan my Change for two days before they shoot me full of drugs that force a Change and make my dragon sick the entire time. There is nothing regular about my life."* There was a pause. *"I used to be fine with that, and then I met you."*

Riyah frowned and changed the pen's rhythm again, drawing a bubble-letter *I* above the broken heart, retracing it over and over. "What do you mean you aren't fine with being yourself anymore? I don't want that. I want you to be happy with you."

*"I mean that I can't..."*

"Can't what, Vyr?"

*"Never mind. I'll be back later."*

"Vyr!"

But she couldn't feel him there anymore. Couldn't feel the dull ache behind her eyes that said he was present.

Runner.

Sadly, she waved her fingers gently through the

air, and without touching the pen, she changed the rhythm again and drew a bubble-letter *U* under the broken heart. She shouldn't feel so strongly about someone this fast. She should be questioning it and running away, but he was here, steady, listening to her, caring about her, wanting to be a part of her day. It wasn't that she was avoiding loneliness either. She hung on every word Vyr said because each seemed important. Like the rest of her life was blurry, but when she and Vyr were together in her head, he was drawn up in fine focus and everything else could burn for all she cared.

The headache came back with a vengeance and she startled when Vyr said, *"I can't have you. Because of what I am, where I am, and all the messed-up parts of my life, I can't have you."*

"Why not?"

*"Because I'm going to lose the dragon, and even if part of me lives, will I really be alive? I'll never fly again, never touch the clouds. I will be earthbound and missing the biggest part of me, and I've seen this. I've seen what happens when shifters lose their animals. They don't come back from that. Usually they beg for death anyway. Even if I live through this and could*

*take you out on a date when I get out...I wouldn't do that to you."*

"Even if it's what I want?"

*"Wants and needs are very different when you are around a man like me, Riyah. You might want me, but you need better than anything I could ever give you."*

"Vyr—"

*"Something's happening. Emmitt's pissed. He's in his observation room yelling at someone on the phone about no more inmates are to be brought to the lower levels. Can you find out what's going on?"*

"Yeah. I'll bring you with me." Riyah bolted out the door, but the hallway was empty and too quiet. What the hell?

She rushed down the tile hallway, her black pumps clicking against the tile floor with every hurried step. She passed the upper level cafeteria, but the group of inmates who were scheduled to be eating right now were nowhere to be seen. Trays were left where they were, food half eaten, cups were overturned, water was dripping down the side of one table. The only person remaining was one of the kitchen staff named Euless.

"What's happening?" she asked.

The old man didn't even look up at her, just continued to sweep up a mess one of the inmates must've made before they left. "New inmates are being brought in," he said in a bored voice.

"Do they lock down the entire facility every time there are new inmates?"

"Nope."

She stood in the open doorway, waiting a few seconds before she got irritated and barked, "Euless! What's going on?"

With a sigh, he leaned on the broom and glared at her. "Nox Fuller and Torren Taylor are here."

Riyah went dumb. There was an entire three-count where she just stood there with her mouth hanging open. "Th-the-the...crew?" They did it?

"Yep. The Red Dragon's crew is gonna be in the same building as him, and everyone is freaking the fuck out. Now if you'll excuse me, I have mixed vegetables to clean off the floor, because that's what I do. I clean up after grown men like they are three-hundred-pound toddlers. I hate my life. Have a good day."

Right. "Okay, see you later, Euless. You're doing a fine job." Riyah speed-walked away, continuing her journey down the long, abandoned hallway. She waited until she passed the camera up in the corner before she whispered, "Vyr."

*"Yeah? I'm here. What's happening? You shut me out. Is it bad?"*

She panted as she jogged in her damn high heels toward the front, barred window. She looked out on the grounds. It was all mowed grass, barbed wire fences, and security towers with a dozen weapons trained on a white transport van.

There were twenty guards, at least, surrounding two men that were stepping out of the van. The first was blond with piercing blue eyes and a full beard. He was laughing like a lunatic, and then he went serious in a flash and lurched at one of the guards, who flinched back. The man laughed again. Even from here, with her less-sensitive human hearing, she could make out his voice clearly. "You should've seen how stupid your face looked, man! It matched your stupid looking hair." He was built like an eighteen-wheeler. Oh, she'd done her research. He was the half-crazed loner grizzly shifter and only son of the Cursed Bear, Clinton Fuller. He was a monster when he Changed and was notorious for fighting everyone and everything. She was staring at none other than Nox Fuller.

Another man followed right behind him, handcuffed just like the blond, wearing a matching tan prison outfit, his neck and arms completely covered in tattoos. He was taller than the other, much wider in the shoulders, with jet black hair, a short beard, and blazing green eyes. He wore a smirk on his face, like he was amused by Nox's trash-talk. Torren Taylor, aka HavoK, aka the new Kong—biggest, baddest, brawler silverback shifter in existence. He was also completely devoted to his best friend and alpha.

"Holy shit," she whispered.

*"What?"* Vyr asked.

"I wish you could see this. They did it."

*"Who?"*

"The Sons of Beasts are here."

She was met with stunned silence.

"Vyr," she murmured, watching the guards escort the two giants into the prison. "Your crew came for you."

# EIGHT

Vyr couldn't breathe. He couldn't breathe, couldn't think straight, couldn't look away from his reflection in the two-way mirror glass. He looked awful, but in his eyes, he saw something he'd only begun to feel recently when Riyah had shown up—hope.

They were here? Torren? Nox? Did Nevada and Candace make it into the girls' side on the west wing of the prison?

*My crew, my crew.*

The dragon clenched inside of him, and it was an unfamiliar feeling. It was desperation from the monster, but he'd never been desperate before. Only angry.

They were here. He let off a shaky breath and closed his eyes, reached out for them with his mind, but they weren't there like Riyah was. He hadn't seen Torren and Nox for six months, and he'd lost the connection to them. If he could just see them face to face, he could fix the broken bond, but there were too many walls between them right now.

The dragon writhed again, doubling Vyr over, and there it was—the anger. He was angry that he'd been cut off from his people.

Torren, Torren, Torren. Nox. Fuck, he wanted out. Needed out. Needed to see them.

*"I just want to see them."*

*"I know."* Riyah. She was still here, still in his head, and he was in hers.

He'd forgotten for a moment.

*"I'm going to see what I can do, okay?"* she said low. *"I'm going to talk to the guards right now and see what I can find out."*

*"Ask how they got in. Ask what they did to land in here. How much time did they each get? Are Nevada and Candace on the women's side? Fuck. Riyah, I don't feel right..."*

*"Vyr, you have to settle down. I can feel you getting*

*riled up, feel the dragon, and you can't do that right now. Go sit on the bed."*

He gritted out, *"I'm not some dog you order to—"*

*"Sit."*

His growl rattled the room and shook the walls. Chips of cement rained down on him and the lights flickered. He was losing it.

*"Steady breaths,"* Riyah whispered. She must be walking where people were because she rarely whispered.

His body buckled, and he went to his knees on the way to the bed. Shit!

*"Vyr, listen—"*

*"Where are you? I need...I need..."* You. He wished he could say that last part, but he couldn't get her hooked on him. Not when he was halfway to hell already. He couldn't drag her with him. She deserved a good life.

*"Babe, stop. Everything is okay. I'm stepping into the restroom...checking stalls...I'm alone. I just called you 'babe.'"*

Her tone sounded shocked, and Vyr huffed out a breath. *"I liked it. I liked it. I'm babe. Fuck, Riyah, listen. You need to get out of the facility."*

*"Oh my gosh. Vyr, I'm coming down to you."*

"No!" he yelled out loud. *"Leave. Please!"*

*"I'm not leaving. You need to stop the Change. Stop it or you'll put me in danger."*

"Riyah," he snarled in an inhuman voice. Already he could feel the cutting pain of his wings scratching to burst out of his back. He could feel his Firestarter begging to be clicked. Could feel the burn of his fire that would explode from his throat. Emmitt called this place hell, but he was wrong. Hell dwelled inside of Vyr. And right now he was having serious trouble keeping the demons inside.

He could feel her coming. She was running toward the elevators. She slid her security card as fast as she could at every reader. He could hear the echo of her heels. Faster, faster. No, no, no.

*"Riyah, please stop! It's been too long. I just want to see them."* He was delirious with the pain, writhing on the ground as he tried to force the dragon back inside. There was chaos as guards surrounded him. Stinging pain as they shot him with the damn meds to try to quell the dragon. Warmth trickled down his lip to his chin. Drip, drip. The Sickening. The Sickening, and Riyah would see him again. But worse, she would

see the Red Dragon, and if she survived him, she would never look at him the same.

*Please*, he begged the dragon. *Let me keep her for a little while. Let me keep her.* He couldn't think. Everything hurt. Someone was singing. Riyah?

She was singing the lyrics to "Baby Got Back." And she was actually doing a pretty decent job of rapping. If his body wasn't on fire right now, he would've laughed.

She was really coming for him. Ridiculous woman didn't understand what kind of danger she was in. This facility couldn't hold the Red Dragon. Oh, the guards thought it could, but they were so fuckin' wrong it was crazy. The people here were still breathing because of the monumental effort he made to keep some semblance of control over his evil side.

And yep, he fully believed the Red Dragon was evil. He didn't feel. He didn't care. He was hunger and vengeance. That's it. That's all. Hunger. Vengeance. Vyr cared very deeply for a few people, but the Red Dragon had cared about literally nothing.

Until Riyah.

*You'll hurt her.* Vyr gritted his teeth and squeezed his eyes closed as his wings ripped out of his body.

*Fuck. Stop. Stop, or you'll kill her and then you'll go back to having nothing and no one.*

A roar screamed from his body, wracking him with a seizure and shaking the room. More cement rained down, and all the lights above him blew. And then there was fire, burning up his throat and illuminating the cell that wouldn't hold his monster.

And as the dragon ripped from him, cell by cell, taking over his mind like black poison... Vyr went to the dark, once again.

# NINE

"Move!" Riyah screamed at the guards blocking the doors to Vyr's cell.

"He isn't stopping, lady! And this place isn't built for a Change like this!"

Riyah barely resisted the urge to flick her fingers and throw the assholes against the wall with the power that pulsed out of her. She needed to keep singing. *Stay calm, keep Vyr calm.*

There was a deafening roar that shook the ground beneath her feet. Shit. She was out of time. She muscled her way between them and slid her card in the reader.

"Mercer! No!"

"Fuck off, Emmitt. If I don't stop him, who will?

Not your goddamn meds! Look what good those did!"

Emmitt's face was red as he stood over her, his hand splayed on the door.

"I can do this," she pleaded.

Emmitt shook his head and shoved a leather pouch against her chest. "This isn't tested, and we only have one dose, but it's supposed to be more potent than the other meds. It could kill the dragon. Kill it before it kills everyone in here."

Riyah wanted to puke. She wanted to puke and then crush Emmitt with her power, but she didn't have time for angry reactions. She had to get in there. She shoved Emmitt's arm off the door and opened it, and what she saw horrified her.

The lights were flickering on and off, buzzing with waves of power. Vyr was still partly human, but he had massive, blood-red, torn and tattered, dragon wings stretching from his back. His face was contorted in rage and anguish and was dripping with blood. He arched his head back and spewed fire at the observation windows on the opposite side of the cell. His eyes were completely vacant, as though he'd shut down completely. But she understood what pain he had to be in to be half Changed and still fighting to keep his skin like this. Fire and magma streaming from a human throat must've been agony. Her heart broke. It broke, simple as that. In this moment, she knew she loved him. She knew she would do anything to make his pain less.

Tears streaming down her face, Riyah ran right for him. He beat his wings, the talons on the ends scratching deep divots into the cement walls as he rounded on her, his eyes blazing silver with elongated pupils. This dragon sure didn't look half-dead.

Terrified but determined, Riyah pushed her legs harder and faster. She heard the clicking of the Firestarter in his chest, but ignored it because she had to trust him. She had to have faith that Vyr wouldn't burn her. That his dragon would let her live. And turning around to run would only get her hurt faster anyway.

Almost there. Almost.

Faster. Her legs were burning, but clutching the leather pouch, she jumped the last few feet and crashed into him just as he opened his mouth full of razor sharp teeth. There were faint scales on his skin and he was turning red, and she was so scared, but she wrapped herself around him and held on for dear life.

When the dragon roared, Riyah's head rang with the sheer volume of it. "Listen. Listen," she begged, voice shaking. "It's me. It's Riyah. And you said you couldn't have me, but you can. Vyr. Red Dragon, look."

His arms went tight around her. Too tight, and his nails dug into her back. Too sharp. He was going to crush her.

"Look!" she screamed, struggling to pull the syringe out of the pouch. "This can kill the dragon. Do you want me to kill it?"

Vyr's face twisted in rage, but he didn't crush her anymore. "No," he rasped out. "Don't kill me."

"Stick him now!" Emmitt screamed under the flickering lights, and the clatter of weaponry sounded. Dozens of rifles clicked, metal on metal, as they were cocked and loaded. There had to be forty guards down here, ready to end Vyr. Ready to end her just for being in the way.

Vyr's hand went to the back of her head as though he was trying to protect her as he blasted a fireball at the densest population of guards. They bolted out of the way, and walls shook with the force of the blast.

Vyr's skin was turning hot against her. Too hot.

"Stick him, or I'm giving the order!" Emmitt screamed from beside the door. He had a high-powered rifle trained on them, too.

Fuck. Fuck. Fuck. She couldn't. She couldn't be the one to kill him. He'd asked her not to. One dose. One shot. Untested. Eyes burning, Riyah eased back and whispered, "Pretend...and then save me."

The dragon's pupils constricted, and the rage on Vyr's face flickered away like a flame being blown out. Confusion took its place. And as she slammed the needle toward his neck, he yelled, "No!"

But Vyr was safe from her. She couldn't hurt him to save herself. She blocked the guards view as best she could and slammed the needle into her arm, no more than an inch from his neck. "Pretend," she pleaded.

And as she emptied that vial into herself, Vyr jerked. A long, low rumble emanated from him as his entire body tensed. With a small whimper, Riyah ripped the empty syringe from herself and dropped it on the floor.

"She did it!" Emmitt shouted. "Back off. Give them space, back off!"

"What have you done?" Vyr gritted out.

"You're mine, and I can't hurt you. Stop the Change. Please. Hide what I've done, or I can't stay here."

"Fuck. Fuck. Riyah." Vyr collapsed to his knees.

Dizzy, she adjusted the sleeve of her white blouse and scrambled away from Vyr as his body shook with power. The air was heavy, full of smoke, and it was getting hard to see, but Vyr looked at her, locked gazes with her, and clenched his teeth. He was on his knees. He blasted his fists against the cement floor as agony roiled in his eyes. His wings stretched the length of the room, his nostrils flared as he heaved breath, and every muscle on his naked torso rippled with tension.

"Sing," he murmured. He rolled his eyes closed, and she picked up where she left off on "Baby Got Back," but softly, her lips barely moving, the words hardly scratching up her raw throat. The smoke made her want to cough, but she resisted the urge so she could continue the song.

And slowly, slowly, Vyr furled his wings and drew them back into his body. The look of pain on his face was heartbreaking. The crimson color left his skin, the scales faded, and as he gritted his teeth in pain, they lost their razor sharpness and turned to blunt human teeth once again. His face softened from the harsh angles and, body shaking, he heaved an exhausted sigh, relaxed back on his bent legs, opened his eyes, and looked down his nose at her. *"You need to go home. I'm here, Riyah. You're gonna get sick from those meds. You need to go. Drink as much water as you can. Call my mom. Get some help at your house. I want someone there with you until this is done."*

"Until what's done?" she whispered.

But the guards rushed Vyr so he couldn't answer her. They yanked his arms behind his back and dragged him away. And then they took her away, too. Away from the man who made her feel safe. From the man who cared enough about her to stop the Red Dragon mid-Change.

"Until what's done?" she asked louder.

Vyr's eyes were haunted as he watched her until she was pulled through the door. He never answered, not even in her head.

And as another dizzy spell took her, she couldn't feel him in her head at all.

Baffled, she watched the guards running this way

and that, guns shouldered, focus on their faces. Her blood was boiling, chilling, boiling then chilling, and she swallowed over and over so she wouldn't retch. Vyr was right. She needed to go home. Right now.

"Excuse me," she murmured, attempting to yank her arm out of a guard's unforgiving grasp.

When she looked up, it was that shifter Vyr had told her to stay away from. Hank Butte. He was staring at her inner bicep with a frown. "Smells like blood," he said in an empty voice. "Looks like it, too."

Indeed, there was a single red drop on the sleeve of her white silk blouse where she'd stabbed herself with the syringe. "Let go of me, asshole," she said as she jerked out of his grasp. She glared over her shoulder as she walked away, just to make sure he wasn't following her. He stood there in the middle of the mayhem watching her leave with a suspicious frown and his head cocked to the side. His eyes were narrowed to glowing blue slits, and chills rippled up her arms. Oh, he knew.

Forcing herself to watch where she was going, she gave that animal her back and quickened her pace. God, she wished she could rip these shoes off and run. She bolted for a trashcan and got sick. She felt awful, could barely think straight, and her head was pounding, but not because Vyr was in there. But because of the medicine running through her veins. She had spells for this. She hadn't practiced them in years, but desperate times and measures. She just needed to get home to those spell books.

But with each step she took trying to escape the prison, nodding to the guards, trying to look like she wasn't in severe pain, it became crystal clear that she wasn't safe to drive home. She made her way through all the security stations, but the last two stopped her and asked if she was all right, probably because she was swaying and had broken out in a sweat. The medicine was to kill a shifter animal, but she was human, so she had no idea what it was doing to her.

She forced a smile, nodded to the guards in the parking lot, and then scrambled into her SUV and fumbled for the burner phone in her glove compartment. She dialed the phone number and groaned as she sped out of the parking lot.

"Are they there?" Clara asked.

"Wh-who?" Riyah stammered weakly.

"Nox and Torren. Riyah, are you okay?"

"No. No, I'm not. I took this medicine I was

supposed to give to Vyr, but I couldn't hurt him. I couldn't hurt him, and now I don't feel... Clara I'm gonna pass out soon." She wasn't going to make it much farther. On the long stretch of road outside of the prison grounds, she pulled over in a rush as her skin went clammy and her stomach rolled with another wave of nausea.

"Riyah, put your car in park."

She fumbled to think clear enough to put it in park, but her hand wasn't working right. "I can't."

"Riyah, yes you can, hon. Put it in park, and then it's okay to go to sleep. I'm getting help to you right now." There was static on the phone and in a muffled voice, Clara told someone to, "Send the girls in. Riyah needs help right now. *Right now.* I don't give a shit. Send them in right now." More static and then in a clear voice, Clara said, "Riyah, are you parked?"

"I think I am," she whispered, melting against the seat. "Tell Vyr I'm sorry. Tell Vyr I'm sorry."

"You did nothing wrong, and you can tell him anything you want tomorrow. Everything is going to be okay."

"He left." Riyah's shoulders sagged, and a sob worked its way up her throat. "I can't feel him."

Clara was still talking, but Riyah couldn't understand what she was saying. And as the edges of her vision shattered inward, she heaved a long sigh, and then Riyah was in the dark, once again.

# TEN

"She sure is sweating a lot," an unfamiliar woman's voice muttered.

"It must be the medicine. I don't think this crap is made for humans."

There was a humorless snort. "You really think she's human? She stinks of magic."

"What?"

"Yeah, can't you smell that bitter scent? Can't you feel it coming off her? That's like…an assload of magic, and she's freaking sleeping. Imagine what she'd be like when she's awake. Beast witch."

"She looks dead."

"Give her more water. Clara said we need to be flushing that shit out of her."

"Well she already puked like a dozen times, so there's that. I feel like I'm in one of those movies, you know? Like the college ones where the girlfriends are holding their hair back while they drunk-puke—"

"Okay, let's talk about anything else. You're making me nauseous."

"That would be the baby making you nauseous, not me. Gotta little gorilla making you green. Eeee! I can't wait to hold him."

Another snort. "It's a her. I'm sure of it. And stop jinxing me. I don't even think I could handle a little Kong. Her father is already both-hands-full."

"And he's in prison."

"So is Nox!"

"Yeah, I was really proud of him for all the dicks he managed to paint all over town in one night. If there is a record for dick paintings, Nox holds it. I drove around counting them. I found eighty-four. Eighty-four, Candace. And those were just the ones I could track down. I'm oddly proud. God, our lives are weird."

"Yep!"

"I wish I'd been successful."

"At being arrested? All you did was drink a bottle

of cheap wine and skinny dip in the public pool. That was never going to get you more than a night in the drunk tank."

"I felt really badass when I did it, though."

There was a pause, and then twin peals of laughter. One of them said, "Check her pulse again. We're almost there, but she looks really bad."

Warm fingertips pressed against Riyah's neck. "She's still with us." As Riyah tried and failed to open her eyes, the stranger murmured in a kind voice, "Poor thing."

"Nevada, don't go all negative on me. She'll be okay."

"I don't just mean about the meds, Candace. I mean, she's the one, right?"

There was a sad sigh. "Yeah. Beaston says she's the one, so she must be."

"I think we should be her friends then. I think she'll need us."

There was a long pause.

Why couldn't Riyah open her eyes? Why couldn't she move? Someone brushed her hair from her face and cradled her head like she was coveted and fragile.

In a hushed murmur, the other stranger said, "I think she'll need us, too."

And then Riyah was in the dark once again.

# ELEVEN

Vyr couldn't feel her.

*"Riyah?"* he asked for the fiftieth time, at least.

Silence.

He couldn't reach her. There was only emptiness where their bond used to be, and now he was truly alone, down here in a cage called The Dungeon. This place had been built with dragons in mind. No one knew about it but Vyr and the guards. This was the prison's well-kept secret. While life went on far above, as the inmates worked, ate, exercised, had time in the yard, fought, showered, visited the commissary, slept...Vyr had just died. Again.

He'd been lying here for hours after Changing back from the dragon, unable to even sit up. Every three weeks for six months, he'd been dragged down to the lowest level of the prison and forced to Change, and it was always the same afterward. He had to burn off the gallon of meds they'd filled him with. His blood was on fire as he lay curled on his side in the middle of the concrete floor. This place was cavernous, much bigger than his cell, to give the Red Dragon space to move, but it was narrow one way and long the other so he could never have enough room to stretch out comfortably and spread his wings. So there he sat for hours on end, blowing fire and magma, unable to move, feeling trapped, feeling claustrophobic, and missing the sky. And by missing the sky he meant that bone-deep, marrow-deep, soul-deep yearning for something he would never see or touch again. Instead, the Red Dragon sat in a steal and cement cage, burning himself with his own fire until he got sick, or gave up and disappeared into Vyr's skin. And for longer and longer periods of time, the dragon would leave completely, and it was just the man named Vyr left. The media called him the Son of the Dragon, but Damon's legacy would end the day the Red Dragon failed to return to Vyr after a Change.

This one was bad. It was the worst one yet. Too

many meds, too little time Changed, and the dragon had given up faster than ever. And now, he'd been lying here for three hours at least, and he still couldn't feel the dragon.

And there was the scrape. He'd landed hard when he Changed back and the side of his forearm was covered in road rash. It seeped still, hours later, and hadn't healed even a little bit. It was a really bad sign.

Body burning from the inside out, Vyr slammed the side of his head on the cement three times and gritted his teeth, wishing to God the dragon would push a pissed-off rumble up his throat, but there was only silence.

There was scratching noises above him. Rats maybe. The dragon hadn't eaten any ashes since Chad, but not even the rats were waking up the monster. Emmitt and the New IESA knew exactly what they were doing. They'd stunted the Red Dragon. Beat him into submission. He'd been defeated, and in this moment, he hated the world he'd been born into. He hated that he was Damon's son. Hated that he'd failed to control the dragon better. Dad always said he didn't try hard enough, but he was far from right. Vyr had devoted his life to training himself to only Change every three weeks. To stop Changes when he was angry. Dad didn't understand. He never had. The Red Dragon wasn't like Damon's monster. Vyr's dragon was completely separate.

And now the New IESA was in some mad-scientist lab above him creating another Red Dragon. Goodbye world if that ever got injected into someone. They had the devil in a syringe, and they didn't even realize it.

*"Riyah?"*

Silence.

God, he wished she was here with him. Vyr's body convulsed again, and another wave of fire burned through his veins. What if she was dead? What if those meds she'd taken into herself had killed her? She was human. Fuck. Fuck. He wrapped his arms around his stomach and curled into a tighter ball to ease the pain.

Maybe that's why he couldn't feel her.

Maybe she was really gone, and if Riyah, that beautiful beacon of hope, was gone, he didn't want to fight anymore.

The whole world said it was better off without him, so at what point did he decide to listen to them?

Everyone thought he was bad, so maybe it was time to accept that he was bad. Maybe he was evil.

The scratching above was getting louder. Vyr tossed the tall ceiling a tired look and then forced himself up on his hands and knees. At least the rats meant he wasn't alone when he did what he had to do next.

Three heaved breaths, and he stumbled to his feet and made his way over to the single observation room with two-way glass because he should see what he suspected.

He stared at the ground as he approached. There was a single light on the other side of the room, a blue one, and it cast the room in dim shadows that looked like moonlight. Always in the dark. The creature of darkness. Everyone was wrong about him. He loved sunlight. He loved flying above the clouds in daylight best. The dragon felt free there, felt good, felt whole.

*"Riyah?"*

Silence.

He came to a stop in front of the mirror glass, and with a steadying breath, he looked up at his haggard face. His stomach dropped to the floor. He would never forget this moment—it was the one where the crack in his stone heart was complete.

Both dragon eyes were frozen in his face now. The Red Dragon was dead. Riyah had tried to save him by taking that medicine, and look what happened anyway.

Vyr inhaled and released an agonized scream as long and loud as he could. Such an ugly, completely human scream. And when it tapered in his throat, he closed his fist and slammed it against the mirror, right at his reflection. The glass shattered outward like a spider web, distorting his hideous face. Good. He would never look in another mirror again. He couldn't, because there was death in his eyes now.

Vyr turned and leaned against the stone wall, cold and damp against his back as he slid down. He slammed his head against it and wondered what it would feel like to cry. He'd never done that before, but if there was ever a time to express that emotion, it was now as he mourned the death of the most important part of himself.

Now, he was nothing at all.

The sound of metal on metal was grating, and Vyr looked up at where the sound was coming from. The rats were really fucking determined in these walls.

He reached out but couldn't feel any guards in the observation room. They usually left him alone when he was recovering. What danger was he now? Sure, he still had his powers from his mom, but they didn't know that. All they knew was the dragon was weakest right after a forced Change.

Something huge fell out of the ceiling, sliding too fast down a rope, and Vyr stared in shock as a familiar face muttered, "Mother fuck-cakes," as he landed hard on his feet on the concrete floor.

Oh, good. The Sickening was giving Vyr visions now. Not just voices in his head or a flash of something that wasn't there. He was having a full-on psychopath moment right now.

Blond hair, blue eyes, twenty pounds of muscle bigger than the last time Vyr had seen him and, "Where the fuck is your beard?" he asked Imaginary Nox.

"Asshole guards made me shave it to make sure I wasn't sneaking in a shank or, I don't know, drugs or something. I look like a twelve year old. I need to grow that shit out quick because Nevada is all about the beard against her poontang. You look like a three-week-old shit."

Imaginary Nox, clad in orange prison garb, approached slowly. Vyr averted his gaze. Even though this wasn't real, he wasn't ready to share what had just happened to him. It was nice to pretend he wasn't alone, though. "How did you get down here?"

"First thing's first. I've been reading a book about how to be a better friend and chapter two said hugs are important."

"Pass."

"Bring it in."

"Nox, I don't want to hug you right now."

"Right now? Okay, so then later we'll hug, after we bond."

Imaginary Nox sat beside him and looked at a stopwatch in his hand. "I have five minutes before I have to get back. Torren is up there fighting like five silverbacks to give me time. Did you know, getting in here without being arrested is impossible? I researched this place for months and couldn't find a single way in, but once you're in? This place is not a well-oiled machine. We have like four people on the inside, two are guards, and your therapist? She's a fuckin' MVP. A goddamn witch. Natural born, too.

Your mom found her and started all of this."

"All of what?"

"Project Rescue the Red Dragon."

"Too late." Vyr's voice echoed hollowly around the room with those two words. He wanted to retch.

"What do you mean?" Imaginary Nox asked softly.

With a sigh, Vyr blinked slowly and rolled his head against the rock, gave Imaginary Nox a clear view of his eyes.

Imaginary Nox's eyes went round, and his lips parted like he wanted to say something, but nothing came out. Red crept up his neck and his face turned to that of fury. "I'm calling this."

"Calling what?"

"This is a goddamn-nough. I fuckin' told them we needed to be doing extraction, not trying to keep you steady while they fuckin' torture you." Imaginary Nox's voice bounced off the walls with the force of his angry words. He flashed a pissed-off glance to the stopwatch in his fist again. "Tell me it's not over. Tell me your eyes don't mean what I think they mean."

"The therapist," Vyr murmured tiredly. "I need to know if she's okay. She took a dose of meds to protect me. I can't feel her anymore. Riyah."

"Okay, the way you just said her name..." Imaginary Nox arched his eyebrows. "Is she yours?"

"Nothing is mine, Nox. That wasn't the life I was born to. I just need to know she's safe."

"Done. I'll find out. Nevada and Candace are on the outside—"

"Why aren't they locked up with us?" Vyr rested his elbows on his bent knees and stared at the blue light across the room. The questions he asked didn't matter because he was making this all up, but damn, it felt good to pretend he was here with one of his crew. He missed Nox.

"Well, because Candace has a little baby Kong in her. I read a book on fetuses. It's like the size of a grain of rice right now. I drew a picture of a tiny gorilla in my dream journal and Nevada thought it was cute as fuck and now I want to put like seventy-three babies in her because she gets all mushy when she talks about them. Plus an army of Noxs would be awesome. Kong and Candace started trying for a little baby for the crew a few months ago. They want a girl, but I'm praying for a boy just to watch them have to raise a mini-Torren. I'm gonna train him to shoot his dad with a crossbow and vandalize shit. Gonna make that little monkey love me more. Anyway, the plan was for us to come in here so you could be close to us, but Torren put his foot down on Candace coming in here pregnant. And my girl…well…she's not the best criminal. She did hang out in the drunk tank in Foxburg for a night though, and I was really fuckin' proud of her." His voice went thoughtful. "If we had more time, I would try to sneak her in for a conjugal visit. I love the challenge of this place. I know the timing of all the guards, all their habits. I know your exact schedule. Fuckin' A-Team. I keep trying to explain I'm the MVP of this crew, and y'all don't believe me. After this, everyone has to stop treating me like the village idiot. I'm way smarter than all of you. Except Nevada. She's a super-hot nerd. Gotta jet, Alpha."

"Don't call me that. I'm no one's alpha."

"False, you are the alpha of the Sons of Beasts. Do you know what this position is doing to Torren while you've been away? He's literally put on forty pounds of muscle, and he fights me every day that ends in Y."

"Bet you love it."

"Fuck yes I love it, but HavoK needs to be controlled, and being in here isn't going to help.

Torren didn't even make it five minutes before he was locked up with a silverback. Our crew can't afford to go backward. We gotta baby on the way now, and half of us are in shifter prison, and one of us looks like a corpse." Imaginary Nox jammed a finger at Vyr. "That's you. I'm talking about you. I'm serious when I say you look like shit. Riyah will never play with your balls if you don't take care of yourself."

Arguing about Riyah not belonging to him was pointless. Nox wasn't really here.

"I have to go. It's hug time."

"Pass," Vyr muttered.

"Fuckface, hurry up, you're going to get me busted, and I'm not leaving until I embrace you. In a manly way."

Vyr wanted to die the rest of the way. Gritting his teeth, he stood up and prepared to hug a ghost because he was in full-on crazy town now. But as Imaginary Nox pulled him in, he was solid and clapped Vyr on the back three times so hard it whooshed his breath out. What the fuck? Vyr froze, his hands held up at Nox's sides. "Nox? You're really here?"

Nox's voice sounded too thick as he said, "I really

missed you, man. I really did. It sucks without you around. There's a huge hole in the crew, and we're struggling to stay steady. Do you know why?"

Stunned, Vyr patted Nox's back and shook his head. "Why?"

"Because you're the glue, Vyr. You always were. And if I ever fuckin' hear you say you're nothing again, I'm going to punch you in the dick. I love you, man. Say it back."

"Nox—"

"I spray-painted one hundred and sixty-nine dicks around the town of Foxburg, Vyr. I signed them all. I got arrested for you. I gave up BJs for a six-month sentence so I could be here for you. Tell me you love me."

Defeated, Vyr muttered, "I love you too, dude."

"Now, tell me Torren is a hairy chode, that he is the worst member of the crew, and that I'm your favorite."

"Nox."

"Worth a try." Nox slapped him hard once more, then spun and jogged to the rope. "Hey, Vyr?"

"Yeah?"

Nox stood there, his face unreadable in the

shadows, holding onto the rope with one hand. "Even if the dragon is gone, you're still important to me. And to Torren, Candace, and Nevada, and a lot people. And I bet you're really important to that girl, too. Riyah? You touch the people who really get to know you."

Huh. Vyr frowned. "You're different than I remember."

"Yeah, Nevada's training me to be normal." Nox snorted. "Just kidding, she would hate me if I was normal. Oh, and Mr. Diddles is still alive. I bought him a girl swan so he could stop humping that stupid duck statue. You owe me thirty bucks. I had to special order her from a feed store. I've named her Mrs. Tittles." Nox slapped his leg, and his single, bellowing laugh echoed as he repeated, "Mrs. Tittles. God, I'm awesome. See you soon, Fuckface." And then Real Nox scaled the rope neatly and disappeared into the ceiling.

Shocked to his core, Vyr was left in the dark, once again. But something small had eased in his middle. Nox had shown up right in the middle of the worst moment of his life and told him he was still important.

And he wanted to tell Riyah about it. He wanted to unload this burden on the girl he couldn't stop thinking about. He wanted to hear it again. That everything would be okay. But he wanted to hear it from her because he was selfish. He wanted those words from Hope, because that's what he sometimes called her in his head. Hope was what she was.

*"Riyah?"*

*"...I'm here."*

Chills blasted against his skin as he went to his knees and arched his head back, closed his eyes in relief. *"Are you okay?"*

*"I will be."* Her voice was so frail in his head. So weak.

*"I wish I could hold you right now. I wish I could take care of you."* God, he wished that more than anything.

*"Me, too. Vyr?"*

*"Yeah, babe?"* She deserved pet names for what she'd done for him. For trying to save him.

*"I was here when you were talking to Nox. Is..."* Her voice dipped to almost nothing in his head. *"Is the dragon really dead?"*

Vyr opened his eyes and stared at the ceiling. And

for the first time in his entire life, a drop of warm water welled up and slid down his cheek. *"Yes."*

Her voice trembled but held honest notes as she murmured, *"Everything is going to be okay."*

He could feel her heartache in his mind. It matched his, and in this moment, he knew he loved her. He knew as long as she was here, in his head, he wouldn't be alone with this.

The crack in his heart filled with something warm, something red. Something that tingled. It was the only thing about him that didn't hurt right now.

Nox had been wrong.

Vyr wasn't the glue.

Riyah was.

# TWELVE

"Everything is going to be okay," Riyah assured Vyr.

*Everything is going to be...okay. Okay. Okay. Everything will be...okay.*

*Riyah!* her mother screamed, *pulling her from Vyr's mind.* "Do it! Baby, look at me." *She fell to her knees, chin lifted high, eyes brimming with tears, but she looked so understanding. So sure.* "Do it now, little witch. Everything is going to be okay."

Riyah jerked awake. She didn't know where she was, but every piece of furniture in the room was floating near the ceiling. Except the bed she was supposed to be lying on was still far below her, resting on the floor. Her hair was floating around her like she was in water. In the open doorway were two women, both with a hand on their chests as they stared silently up at her with similar, uncertain gazes.

It was like this sometimes when memories of what she'd done scratched at her mind. The power she kept so secret, so hidden, came out in her sleep. "I'm sorry," she murmured as she lowered herself and the furniture back to the floor.

She turned, landed on her tiptoes, and looked down at herself. She was wearing a black crop top that said *Gem's* across the front and a pair of purple-sequined sparkle shorts. "Uh, what am I wearing?"

The curvy brunette lowered her eyes to the floor and spoke in the softest, most timid voice Riyah had ever heard. "S-so this is gonna sound weird, but we've decided you're going to be our friend, and friends like things that match. Candace was in the middle of teaching me how to pole-dance...sooooo..." She looked down at her own green sparkly shorts, then at Candace's blue ones. "So we dressed you like us today. I'm Nevada. Fox shifter. Mate to Nox Fuller and part of the Sons of Beasts Crew. Vyr is my alpha." She ghosted Riyah a look and lowered her eyes to the floor again.

"And I'm Candace," said the lean and leggy woman with auburn hair and false eyelashes. "Baby momma and mate to Torren Taylor, and Vyr is also my alpha. So you know...don't kill us with your witchcraftery because, by default, we really are friends. You like Vyr, and Vyr likes us. We think. He's hard to read sometimes. He might actually hate everything and everyone, but he hates us the least, so it counts. Your other clothes smelled like prison so we had to change you, girl. I get nauseous easy nowadays."

"Morning sickness," Nevada whispered.

"Congratulations on the baby," Riyah blurted, barely resisting the urge to cover her exposed stomach with her arms.

"Congratulations on being a badass with telekinetic powers," Candace said with a nod of respect. "I mean, you're terrifying as hell, but as long as you keep us on your good side, we're totally cool with you being Vyr two-point-oh. Also, if I ever have to move, I would like to hire you so you can just do it for me, Mary Poppins style."

Riyah snorted. She'd never been compared to Mary Poppins before. More often, if someone saw a hint of what she could do, they made the sign of the devil and scurried away.

"S-so do you always sleep like there is a demon in you?" Nevada asked, attention still on the floor.

"She means with the floating and flying furniture. Also, it stinks like magic in here so I'm just gonna plug my nose, but it's not me being rude. I'm a tiger shifter, and my senses are all jacked up with this baby Kong in my belly." Candace plugged her nose but smiled brightly.

"Um, no. I don't do that often. How long have I been out?"

The women looked at each other and then back to Riyah. "A day. You missed Vyr's Change. Clara has been calling non-stop, checking on you, but there was no waking you up to be there for him. You were really, really sick. She understood."

"I have to tell you something," she murmured, sinking onto the bed. "Since we're friends and wearing matching sparkly shorts..." Her voice shook so she swallowed hard before she tried again. "I can talk to Vyr. In my head."

Candace's eyes went round as dinner plates. "Whoa. So you really are Vyr two-point-oh."

"We have some similar powers, but I'm no dragon." She clutched the covers under her hands. "And now, neither is Vyr."

Nevada jerked her gaze off the floor. "What do you mean?"

Riyah's face crumpled just thinking about it. She couldn't look them in the face when she told them what had happened to Vyr. Couldn't. Shame heated her cheeks. "Clara wanted me to keep Vyr steady enough to keep the dragon for the rest of his six-month stay in that prison."

"And?" Candace asked.

"And today the dragon died."

"Oh, my God," Nevada uttered. She stood frozen before she turned and left. Just...left. And moments later, even with her dull human senses, Riyah could hear the woman crying in the other room.

Candace just stood in the door frame, arms crossed over her chest, watching Riyah. "I have to tell you something, too. Something that will be hard to hear."

"Okay," Riyah said, feeling awful. All she wanted to do was go to Vyr and be there for him.

"After we watched that video you did, the one

where Vyr asked for his crew to come to him? We got a call from the seer of the Gray Backs, Beaston. Have you heard of him?"

"Yes," Riyah whispered, stunned. "Clara told me about him. She said he can see things kind of like we can."

"He can see across the veil. Can see ghosts, but more than that, he can see things that will happen in the future. Good things and bad things. All things he can't change. His son is the same as him. When one of them has a vision that can affect everyone? It's a big deal. But when both of them have the same vision, over and over and over…everyone pays attention." Candace rested her head on the doorframe and looked so sad as she said the next part. "You're the one who will revive the Red Dragon, but afterward, Beaston and his son Weston both see the same thing."

"What do they see?" Riyah asked.

"Fire. Fire everywhere."

# THIRTEEN

"Did you leave fingerprint bruises on my leg on purpose?" Riyah asked in the darkness.

*"Yes,"* came Vyr's immediate reply.

"I've wondered that since you kissed me."

*"I'm gonna kiss you again someday."*

"Ahh, you're back to fighting."

*"No. What are you doing right now?"*

"Lying in bed," she said. "Nevada and Candace are staying at a hotel next door to my apartment complex until we get things figured out."

*"What things?"*

"You'll see," she said with a smile. She did her best to keep the plans a secret. Not because she wanted to keep things from Vyr, but because she wanted to give him an entire day of surprises tomorrow. He deserved a good day after what he'd been through.

*"Why are you so nice to me?"*

"Because I like you."

*"You like, like me?"*

"I have a crush."

*"Fuuuuck. I wish I could've watched your lips when you said that."*

"What are you doing right now?"

*"You don't want to know."*

With a frown, she sat up in bed. "I want to know everything."

*"They never brought a bed into The Dungeon, and they haven't taken me back to my cell yet. So...I'm lying on the concrete floor, hands linked behind my head, staring at a dark ceiling, and wishing to God I was in your apartment, lying next to you."*

"Vyr," she whispered.

*"Stop. At least we have this."*

Riyah drew her knees up to her chest. "You feel important."

There were three beats of silence and then, *"So do you."*

"I want to tell you something I've never told anyone. I want to tell you about what you saw in my head."

*"It wasn't your fault."*

"Maybe not, but it has always felt like it."

Vyr gave a mental sigh. *"I'm ready."*

"Once upon a time, there was a witch and her daughter, and the witch had a husband who was a good man. The little witch was lucky, but sheltered because she had powers she sometimes couldn't control, just like her mother. But by hiding, they attracted attention from a crew of very rare shifters that lived in the territory. Polar bears. They were trying to keep quiet. Keep from having to register like the government was making all the other shifters do. They would visit us and tell us to leave the territory because they were afraid we would attract attention. But we had nowhere to go. Eventually, the visits got scary. It wasn't just about protecting themselves anymore. It's like they could taste the magic, and it drew them in. Made them crazy. When they shifted, they would come closer and closer. And at nights, we could hear them roaring. Closer, closer, closer. The little witch's father approached the crew to ask them to stay away, but he didn't come back. And that same night, the roaring came right up to the trailer. The little witch's mom scooped her up and ran out the back door just as the front door caved in. And they ran into the woods as fast as they could. And the little witch didn't know she was doing it, but her fear was leaching power from her mother. So when her mother turned to defend them from the bears, she had nothing. No power."

Riyah's voice broke on the last word, so she paused and swallowed hard so her voice would come out steady again. "The little witch watched as the white bears ran through the trees. Two of them landed on her mother, and there were screams. And the little witch's body was pulsing with power. The more scared she got as she screamed for her mother, the more the power burned to escape her. Fuck." She wiped her damp cheeks fast and shook her head hard. *Just say it.* "My mom, she got a break from the attack, but I was surrounded. It was a big crew, and the bears were just...massive. She struggled to her feet and turned, and whatever she saw in me, it took the fear from her eyes. She was crying and bleeding, so much, but she told me, 'Riyah! Do it!' I was so scared of the white bears, but Mom said, 'Baby, look at me.' And she fell to her knees and said, 'Do it now, Little Witch. Everything is going to be okay.' And I screamed because the power hurt as it came out of me."

Riyah swallowed a sob. "I decimated everything within a square mile, my mom included. So you see, Vyr, you think you're a monster. And others think you're a monster because you eat people. But they don't realize you see the bad ones. You see evil, and you do something about it to satisfy your dragon. You protect your people at great cost to yourself. I, on the other hand, destroyed the person I loved the most. And she was good. Pure. Kind. You aren't a monster, Vyr. I am. I see you. I know what it was like for you. You grew up different from everyone else. You had to hide all the real things about yourself. You had to appear tough, even when people hurt you with their words or the thoughts you could hear. You became steel. That scares other people, but for me, I love that I get to see past the steel. It makes me feel less alone."

*"You're never alone. Not anymore, Riyah."*

"I will be if you quit fighting. So don't. I don't want to go back to the way it was. I want you to kiss me again. I want you to touch me, hug me, and when my world is crashing and burning around me, I want you to be the one to tell me everything will be okay. Promise me."

*"A promise like that should be made in person. What are you wearing?"*

Baffled, she looked down at her oversize T-shirt. "Uuuh...sexy negligee?"

*"Liar. Take off whatever you're wearing."*

"Even my pink and black polka dot panties? I should tell you now I'm terrible at sex talk."

*"No, Badass Princess, you just did good. I can imagine those polka dot panties. They're already way better than the brown ones."*

"Soft beige. And I'm wearing an extra-large, brown, threadbare root beer shirt that I bought with ten Pepsi bottle caps a decade ago."

*"I'm getting a boner."*

Riyah giggled. "Zip it," she murmured, grateful that he was lightening up their conversation after her admission about her mother.

*"I'm serious. Okay, imagine it. I'm lying right next to you. Kick the covers off."*

With a grin, she did and then laid back. "Covers

are off. Root beer shirt is still on."

*"I'm running my fingertips up your ankle, up your shin lightly to your knee, over the curve to your thigh, up, up until I reach the hem of your shirt. I hesitate for just a second, and I'm looking right at you. I slide my hand under the shirt and grip your hip. Hard. I dig my fingers in and turn your body toward me."*

She turned and she could imagine him here, looking at her with those blue, human eyes, because here, in their world, she wanted to pretend he still had the dragon. She wanted to pretend they weren't both damaged beyond repair. Tonight, she just wanted to be a regular girl in love with a boy.

*"I hook a finger in the elastic of those panties and, slowly, I drag them down your hip, just enough to make room for my hand to slip between your legs."*

"Okay, this is really sexy," she murmured, feeling flushed as she dragged her fingertip over her hip.

*"We're just getting started."*

She swallowed hard and murmured, "You don't have a shirt on, and I'm running my palm down your chest, down your abs..."

"Mmmm," Vyr murmured in a sexy, sultry groan. *"Grab my dick. It's so hard right now. I want to see your hand on it, stroking it. Slow. Do it slow at first."*

"I wrap my hand around you and push down, down, and you roll your hips, encouraging me. You keep us slow."

*"I'm cupping you between your legs, and you're so fucking wet. I can feel it on my fingertips, and I'm desperate to be moving inside of you. My other hand...I've got it on your throat. I'm gentle about it. You give me this sexy, wicked smile because you know I won't hurt you. You know I'm going to make you feel good. And I push my fingers inside you. Wet. So warm, I'm pushing my dick harder into your hand now because I'm getting desperate."*

"I bite your bottom lip to play. I like that you're getting rougher but staying in control. I can feel a drop on the head of your cock when you pull back, and I want to taste it."

*"Fuck. Fuck, do that. Taste it."*

"You grip my hair, not hard, but with enough pressure that I know what you want. You pull your fingers out of me and push my face down toward your hips. And I slide my mouth over you."

Vyr's breath quickened, and God, she loved this.

*"Keep going."*

"I put just enough pressure on you as I slide my lips down you as far as I can take, my hand gripping you, moving with my mouth. Slow at first, like you want. Slow, slow, and then your hand goes tight in my hair, so I suck on you faster. Faster and deeper, and you're moving your hips with me.

*"Touch yourself."*

Feeling wicked, she slid her hand down the front of her panties and pushed two fingers inside herself. She made a soft noise when she went deep enough to bump her clit. "Warm. Wet."

*"Oh my God, Riyah, I'm close. I want to finish in you though, so I pull out of your mouth and push you onto your back. Spread your legs for me. Do it now."*

She spread her legs wider and arched her back against the mattress, pushed her fingers into herself again and again.

*"I'm between your legs now, kissing your lips but the head of my cock is right there, thrusting shallow. Barely pushing into you. Beg me."*

"Please, Vyr," she whispered.

Vyr groaned a sexy sound, and she could imagine him stroking himself, thinking of her. This was the hottest thing she'd ever been a part of. *"Fuck, I'm going so deep. I'm not gentle now. I'm rough and sliding into you fast, hard. Deep. Soooo deep. I'm close."*

"Me, too," she whispered as the pressure built between her legs. "I wish you were really here. I want to feel you. Sooo bad."

Vyr groaned again, and his breath was coming quick now. "*Riyah*," he gritted out, just as she came.

Her body shattered around her fingers with such intensity she curled in on herself and screamed his name.

*"I'm throbbing so hard, so deep in you right now."* His breath hitched, and she could imagine how warm it would be if he was spilling into her.

Her body twitched as her orgasm dragged on and on.

*"You're so beautiful. You know that, right?"* Vyr asked.

Riyah smiled as her aftershocks slowed and faded. "You make me feel beautiful."

*"Good. I'm holding you now because you'll want to flinch away from what I have to say. I'm hugging you tight, and you're resting your head against my chest. I see you too, Riyah. I can see how good you are. I've read thousands of people over a lifetime, and no one*

*has felt like you. I can immediately tell if a person is good or not. Doesn't matter that they're afraid of me. Everyone's afraid of me. Fear is projected at me with this...dark energy, and I had to learn to absorb it. It's poison and I'm a sponge, and I had to learn to just take it all into me. I hate fear the most. My soul can taste it, and it sickens me. But you...you're light. You pull those shadows out of me and make each day easier. What happened to your mom—"*

"You mean what I did to my mom?" she whispered in the dark.

"No...I mean what happened to her...that wasn't your fault. Blame that fuckin' crew if you want, but not yourself. Your mom made a sacrifice. She wanted you to be okay, and she told you to let go of what she'd given you. With each day you blame yourself? You take away from that sacrifice. Honor her, Riyah. Live a full life for both of you."

She was tearing up a bit, but it wasn't from heartbreak. She felt such potent relief that someone was giving her sanctuary from the guilt she'd carried for so long. But Vyr's tone confused her. "Why does it sound like you're saying goodbye?"

"Oh, I'm not. You're stuck now, Badass Princess.

*You lost your broken dragon, but you gained a broken man. You're mine. I'm yours. And when I get out of here, I'm going to try to be okay someday. For you."*

"Is that a promise you'll fight for us?"

*"Yeah, Riyah. For you, I'll fight. Now go to sleep. I'm going to stay right here until you do. I'm not leaving you to the darkness. I'm here. Until you tell me to leave, I'm right here."*

She smiled sleepily. "I'm here, too. You aren't in the dark either."

*"Riyah?"*

"Yeah, Vyr?"

*"Everything is going to be okay."*

# FOURTEEN

The video footage of Vyr discovering the death of his dragon broke Riyah's heart. She couldn't even help her tears as she watched him stare at his reflection in The Dungeon. He screamed the most raw, heart wrenching sound she'd ever heard, and then he blasted his fist against the glass. He looked disgusted, then ripped his gaze away from the broken glass and slid his back down the wall. For the rest of her life she would never forget the agonized look on his face. She didn't want to see it, but Emmitt was showing all the lower level teams how the cameras shorted out suddenly.

There was a three-man technical team involved, but so far, no one could figure out what was happening with the glitches in the lighting and cameras. Unfortunately, Emmitt kept playing the footage of Vyr breaking over and over and over again until it glitched, but by this point, Riyah couldn't watch it anymore. The lights flickered, and the television blacked out, and this time it wasn't Vyr's power that was the problem. It was hers.

Shit. She had to settle down.

"Seriously?" Emmitt yelled. "We can't even have a technical meeting without technical difficulties? I want this figured out! Now!"

Over a dozen people went scurrying for the door. Riyah was standing against the back wall, her arms crossed over her chest as people rushed past her. All were leaving but Emmitt and Hank Butte, who was sitting at a table near her, leaned back in the chair, staring at her with a feral, empty smile.

"Glitch, glitch, witch, witch," he murmured softly. Emmitt didn't seem to hear it from where he was trying to get the television working again.

"There was something going on with the ceiling right before it cuts," Emmitt muttered.

But Riyah couldn't take her eyes off Butte's blazing ice-blue gaze. He wasn't even trying to hide the shifter in him.

He had her card punched, so she felt zero percent rude asking, "What are you?"

"I knew of a witch once. A kid. She took everything from me. I suppose I should thank her, though. She made me what I am." Butte stood and strode with inhuman grace to the door. And just as he passed her, he locked her in a hate-filled gaze. "Polar bear. Not many of us left thanks to you, bitch. Bitch, bitch...witch, witch." He curled his lips back for a moment, exposing sharp canine teeth, and then he left Riyah there, feeling like she was right back in the woods with her mom all those years ago.

She couldn't breathe. Her lungs burned for air, but she couldn't drag any in. She stood there frozen. The lights buzzed and dimmed to nothing, recovered and dimmed again. One of the fluorescent bulbs popped, and glass rained down on the tables below. Before Emmitt could turn around, she bolted from the room.

Butte was gone, and she was alone in the hallway. She needed to kickstart the plans. There were a lot of moving parts, and Butte was going to be a problem. Fuck another six months for Vyr. For Torren and Nox, too. She needed the crew extracted as soon as possible, but they couldn't just do a jailbreak. Things had to happen so Vyr could really be free, not spend his life on the run. Butte threw a huge wrench in things though, and now Riyah's time in this prison was limited. Butte could out her at any time.

She bustled to her office, but when she got there, her door was open a crack. Furious, she threw it open to find Butte with his arms locked on the desk, staring at her tablet.

"You sure have your security settings up high on this," he murmured remorselessly.

"Yeah, so dickholes like you can't log in and see my online shopping bills," she said coolly. "Now get the fuck out of my office before you end up like your crew."

Fury flashed in his glowing blue eyes as he pushed off the table. He picked up the tablet and chucked it against the wall so fast, he blurred. The tablet shattered into a hundred pieces. He rushed her, but before he got to her, she lifted her hand, palm facing him, and froze him in his tracks. And as he stood there, helpless and with a rage written onto every facet of his face, she told him how it really was.

"Your crew killed my dad when he came to ask them to leave us alone. They just...mauled him. The police found him in pieces. And then your crew came after me and my mom, and I lost her, too. We're fuckin' even, you self-righteous asshole. And if you ever come at me again like you just did? You will be ash and dust." She twitched her fingers, and he flew out her door and slammed into the wall on the other side of the hallway so hard the wall caved inward around his body. With the flick of her fingers, she slammed her door, locked it, and closed the blinds. She didn't give a single fuck what his reaction was to her. He could throw his tantrum elsewhere. Right now, she had a call to make.

Hands shaking, heart fluttering, chest heaving, she pulled the new burner phone out of her purse and dialed Clara's number. It was Damon who picked up, though. "What's happened?"

"Our timeline just changed. Beck Anderson of the Boarlanders. Can we trust her to get things rolling?"

"She's the best at shifter relations. She's got teams across the country waiting for the word from us, and Cora Keller of the Breck Crew is a well-known news anchor who can have any video footage you collect edited within hours. She can get us in front of a big audience. We will go to war publicly with the New IESA and what has been done to Vyr the second you say 'go.' We're all here. The Ashe Crew, the Gray Backs, the Boarlanders, the Lowlanders, the Breck Crew, the Bloodrunners, the Blackwings, Red Havoc, all of them, watching you. Waiting on you."

"I will testify to everything. I'll expose exactly what they are doing here, and I'll get footage today, but everything needs to happen now."

"Right now?"

"Right fuckin' now, Damon. Your son lost the dragon. He lost it, and he's trying to stay strong for me, but I saw the footage of his face when he found out the dragon was dead. He won't be okay in here much longer, and I can't watch this anymore. I..."

"Say it."

"I love your son. I've been watching them break him, but it stops now."

"Okay. Okay," he repeated. "Riyah, you have to stay safe while we're handling things on the outside. It's about to get real tense in there, and you are a new hire. They're going to be looking for a mole, and they're going to look right at you first. If we lose you, we have no platform to call the shifters to arms. Do you understand?"

"Yes. You need me to testify. You need me to get good footage of what's happening in here. Need me to expose everything from a firsthand account. Get Vyr, Nox, and Torren out of this place free and clear. And to do that, I have to be okay."

"Yes. And also…"

"Also what?"

"My son…you love him. You're trying to help him…and because of that, you're very important to me. You have the fealty of the Blue Dragon. I know what happened to your family. I've known about it for a long time, and I can guess how you must feel. You aren't alone in there, though. You have Vyr, you have the Sons of Beasts, but you also have all of us. Riyah, you have the biggest crews in the world at your back. We're ready. You are commander on this. Even if your man is down right now, you have dragon's fire at your disposal. Me, Dark Kane, Roe, Harper, Diem…we'll blow that place out of the water if harm comes to any of you. Use us the second you need us. I'll call Beck and Cora right now. Turn on the news tonight and see what you set into motion. We're going to get you all out of there. We just need time, and until we can, you have to keep the Sons of Beasts safe." His voice dipped to a whisper. "Keep my boy safe." And then the line went dead.

The lights buzzed and dimmed to nothing, and Riyah had to close her eyes and focus to stop the power from streaming out of her. Something was happening. She was getting stronger. Maybe it was being threatened by a polar bear shifter again, but she suspected it had more to do with Vyr. Was she leaching power from him like she'd done to her mom? Or was he giving it to her?

Eyes still closed, she concentrated and let the wall down, let Vyr into her mind. "I'm not even using spells to give me more power, and I'm getting stronger," she whispered.

*"Good,"* Vyr said. *"You're strong enough to control it, you know? I can see you are. They're bringing me up from The Dungeon. Can I see you?"*

And just like that, all the stress of the meeting, Butte, the phone call, and the pressure of everything lifted. Vyr had that uncanny ability to make things seem doable, even when they felt impossible.

"Last night when we talked, when we

were…together…you seemed okay."

*"You saw video?"*

"Yes. You broke the window when you saw your reflection."

*"I want to protect you from that stuff."*

"I think…" She looked down at the broken heart doodle she'd drawn the other day. At the bubble letters that spelled *I love you.* "I think it's time to stop protecting each other from the real stuff and lean on each other instead. Let me shoulder it with you. I'm tough."

*"And getting tougher. I can feel it. Beautiful Badass Princess."*

Pain blasted through her head and landed behind her eyes.

*"Butte?"* Vyr growled. *"Butte tried to hurt you?"*

"Heeey, don't steal memories. That's against the rules."

*"How would you like me to kill him?"*

"If it comes down to that…with fire."

*"Riyah,"* Vyr warned. *"I don't have that anymore, and I don't want to keep talking about it. That won't help me. It'll keep me on my knees."*

"Here is a memory for you," she murmured,

recalling the phone call with Damon. "Your dad didn't put you in here without a plan." She winced as stinging pain rippled through her head. Vyr was quiet. Too quiet. "Are you okay?"

*"I feel betrayed. I'm quiet about it, but my dad…my own father…helped put me here. I've been down here for six months thinking he didn't care. Been down here for six months going through hell, hurting every day, thinking I'm expendable to the man I want to be proud of me the most. And he tells you right away about his plans, but gives me no explanation. You want real? No. I'm not okay."*

"I'll be here when they bring you up from The Dungeon. I'll be here always, okay?"

But the headache was gone, and so was Vyr.

Crap. She dug around her purse for the tiny plastic baggie Nevada and Candace had given her this morning and pulled out a tiny video camera. It was disguised as a gold star sticker, so she stuck it on the back of her clipboard and pressed it once. There was a soft beep that told her it was on, and then nothing. It just looked like she'd decorated her clipboard, and now she had twenty-four hours of memory on this little camera to gather footage against this prison and against the New IESA. Riyah rushed to put the burner phone in her purse, locked it in the bottom drawer of her desk, locked her office, then speed-walked toward the elevators that would take her down to the lower levels. In a daze, she swiped her security card at each reader and moved deeper and deeper toward the lair.

She was still walking in that daze when someone knocked insanely loud on one of the windows of the cells. Riyah was shocked to see Nox Fuller and Torren Taylor in one of the all-white rooms. Nox was plastered against the window with the biggest grin on his face, and Torren was lying in the middle of the floor, all spread out, looking like a giant starfish. The dark-haired man was massive. And so was Nox, who was knocking again. He made a series of hand gestures, but Riyah couldn't understand sign language. "I don't know sign language," she said loud enough for him to hear through the glass.

"He doesn't know sign language either," Torren said from the floor. "He just likes to annoy everyone and pretend he does."

She studied the picture of the smeared red penis someone had drawn on the back wall. "Is that...is that drawn in blood?"

"It's not weird," Nox said through the glass. "Torren and I got in a fight, and I had extra blood. This room is fuckin' boring. All white? Whoever the decorator of this place is, I want their name and number. I have formal complaints."

Riyah huffed a laugh—the first one today.

"You're Riyah, right?" Nox asked.

The behemoth on the floor rolled his head toward her and narrowed his eyes, then stood smoothly and came to stand beside Nox.

"I am. I can schedule a counseling session with you if you feel like you need to talk," she said smoothly, in case the camera up in the corner could pick up audio.

"Oh, I feel super feely," Nox assured her. "I probably need, like, thirty years of counseling. Can you pencil me in? Torren, too? He's super-violent right now and needs to talk about his feelings also."

"Yep," Torren said blandly. "I have lots of feelings."

With a sympathetic nod, she said, "I completely understand. It's a big adjustment coming into shifter prison. How did you two end up in the lower levels?"

Nox grinned. "Fighting."

"Each other?" she asked.

"Fighting everyone. This is like time-out for the super baddies, huh. They gave us lunch, and I was excited because I thought it was mashed potatoes, but nope. It was gruel. I mean it tasted fuckin' delicious, but it was definitely not mashed potatoes. Can you put in a request for steak? I like mine rare. Like...just walk the cow by the fire. And we need some veggies so we don't get scurvy."

"Scurvy. Like what pirates used to get when they didn't have enough vegetables on long trips...stealing..."

"Say booty," Nox said through a grin.

Riyah sighed and repeated, "Booty."

"Yep! Have you talked to the girls?"

"Shhh." She shushed him low through clenched teeth as she gave a quick glance up at the camera.

"Oh, that camera has no audio. We got put in this cell on purpose."

"On...purpose." What the heck? "You know how to work the system in here?"

"Hell, yeah. When you request the steak, can you ask Euless about it in the cafeteria? He's one of ours.

He won't spit in it."

"Oh." She blinked slowly. "Sure."

"Thanks, Ri-Ri," Nox said.

Torren rolled his eyes and muttered an apology for Nox.

"I'm going to see your alpha."

Torren perked up and pressed his hands on the glass. "How is he?"

"Dude, I already told you he's fine," Nox said. To Riyah though, Nox shook his head slightly and gave her a warning look with his eyes.

"He's doing okay, considering," she said. It wasn't a lie. She knew better than to try those with shifters.

"Considering what?" Torren asked, straightening his spine.

Nox was standing there with his eyes gone round, lips pursed, and shaking his head jerkily. So she shouldn't tell Torren that Vyr lost the dragon?

"I'll ask about the steak. See you soon," she blurted out and walked away without looking back.

On one of their late-night talks, Vyr had spoken of Torren like he was a flesh-and-blood brother, and if Nox didn't want Torren to know how bad it was for Vyr, she needed to listen. She'd done her research on

Vyr's crew before she accepted this job, just to see what she was in for. And to get a better feel for Vyr. The people an alpha gathered under him said a lot about the kind of person they were. Vyr had gathered some very loyal friends. And Torren had pledged himself to protecting the Red Dragon from age seven. If he was having a violence problem in here, she didn't need to set him off with gory details. That would only get him and Nox hurt in that little cell. She made a mental note to bring Nox in for counseling first to better understand how to handle Torren's session afterward.

She swiped her card at Emmitt's observation station, careful to keep her clipboard hugged to her chest so the camera could catch everything.

"What are you doing here?" he muttered from his rolling chair as he watched footage of two guards escorting Vyr up an elevator. Vyr stared directly into the camera, and it hurt to witness the emptiness there. Two dragon eyes, frozen into his face. Vyr swayed with the movement of the elevator, unblinking. The scar on his head was stark and red, and he had a black eye that wasn't healing.

"What happened to his face?"

Emmitt shrugged. "Dragon extraction was successful. Now he doesn't heal like he used to."

"The dragon is...dead?"

"Dead as a doornail. Look at those eyes. He'll look like a freak for the rest of his life, but the world is safe."

*Stay calm. Stay steady.*

"I guess I'm still confused about this place," she murmured, sitting in the other chair. She rested the clipboard on her thighs and swung back and forth slowly in the chair. "Do we have to take the animals out of all the lower level shifters?"

"Nah, just the ones we want to duplicate. And when we get monsters like Vyr, it's better for everyone if they just disappear. He's helpless now. Look at him. You saw those videos of him burning Covington to the ground? And him blowing up police cruisers the day Butte brought him in? Well...now he's just a man."

"Who was sentenced to a year in prison. Not a cleansing."

"Who's gonna miss the Red Dragon?" he gritted out, ripping his gaze from the screen and glaring at her. "You?"

"I'm paid to be empathetic, Emmitt. These aren't animals. They're people."

"Chhhh. Too sympathetic for your own good. We saved your life by killing that demon. You should be thanking us. That's six months of work—"

"You mean six months of torture."

"What the fuck is wrong with you, Mercer?" Emmitt yelled. "You knew the drill coming down here. Fuck! Today we're celebrating. Literally, we're throwing a ding-dong-the-dragon-is-dead party, and if you shit on our parade, I'm taking it to the higher-ups. You don't belong down here. This is where the real work happens. Shut your fuckin' trap, bitch, and be happy there's no need to worry about Vyr's fire anymore. All of our lives just got a ton easier."

"And his life?"

"Is over. He's one person, though. One. He's an easy sacrifice."

Riyah swallowed bile and tried to compose her face as Emmitt pushed the intercom and said, "The lair is clear. Bring him on in."

"Since the dragon is dead, I think he should have more privileges now."

"Good God, woman, what are you talking about?

This is prison, not the Ritz."

"Exactly, and all the inmates upstairs are getting meals together and yard time together. They aren't alone all the time. He can't even shift anymore, right? Look at his face, Emmitt. Really look at it. Someone hit him, and he's not healing."

"What about 'his life is over' is confusing to you?" Emmitt was staring at her like she'd lost her mind. "There will be an accident in here. Vyr isn't getting out. Keep pushing, and you won't get out of here either. You're feeling mighty risky to the New IESA program right now."

"Don't you threaten me. I took the same oath of silence you did. I'm allowed to ask questions, though. That's my job to get the inmates in a safer mindset to make your job easier. That's what I'm paid for. Vyr is helpless, like you said, yet the program still wants him eradicated."

"Because we're exposed the second he tells anyone what it's like in here!" Emmitt barked. "And it's not just my ass on the line, or Butte's, or any of these guards, or the New IESA. It's your ass on the line, too. You get that, right? You understand you were a part of this? Maybe the biggest part. Think about it, Mercer. You came in, settled the dragon immediately, we all saw it. You were a fucking monster-whisperer, stuck that needle in him, gave him that monster dose of dragon killer, and then the Red Dragon died. You're just as guilty as the rest of us, if not more. His eyes being frozen like that?" Emmitt jammed his finger at the screen where Vyr was still staring directly at the camera. "Your fault. That black eye not healing? Your fault. The accident that will happen? Also your fault." Every accusation felt like the lash of a whip against her heart. "Careful where you step around here, Princess. There's landmines everywhere, and I'm the biggest one. No more questions. Vyr doesn't get special privileges. He's done. Give me two days, and we'll be tossing the corpse. And daddy dragon can't do shit about it because he was the one who helped put Vyr in here in the first place. We. Win."

We win? The New IESA wins? Winning by murder. Disgusting. She dared Emmitt to try for an "accident." She would turn him to ash in a second. Riyah smiled coolly. "Whatever you say, boss."

"Fuckin' attitude," Emmitt muttered, giving his attention back to the computer. "This is why I told them not to hire girls down here. Sentimental idiots, all of you."

She could literally pop his head like a grape right now and never lose an ounce of sleep.

*"As much as I would love to see that, I don't want you skipping over to the dark side, Badass Princess."*

Riyah let off a relieved sigh and embraced the headache. That pain meant she wasn't alone. She would take a headache for the rest of her life if it meant Vyr was okay. Which...from the looks of him as the guards brought him in, clad in handcuffs and chains around his ankles, limping badly and sporting a completely dead look on his face, he wasn't okay, just like he'd said.

She wanted vengeance. She wanted justice. She wanted to punish every guard who had ever laid a hand on Vyr or shot him with drugs or operated on him. Soon.

Right now, she just needed to be here for Vyr and bring him back from the brink. At some point between last night and now, he had quit fighting completely. She didn't know what had happened, but she would find out if she had to scour every inch of video footage.

The camera streamed directly to Damon's technical team, so she took the clipboard with her as she left the observation room. At the door, Emmitt asked, "Where are you going?"

"To welcome Vyr back to his lair." She gave him a ghost's smile. "I'm gonna make his last days bearable."

"Why?" he gritted out.

"Because it's the right thing to do." Riyah let the door swing closed behind her and barely resisted the urge to collapse that observation room on top of Emmitt.

She made her way through the two card scanners and pulled open the door to Vyr's lair.

The guards were just leaving. They gave each other a high five. She didn't even what to know what that was about because she was really close to snapping already. Even she could smell the magic coming off herself right now.

Vyr's eyes went wide as he watched her approach with her clipboard clutched to her chest. "Riyah, you look hot as fuck, but your hair is floating, and there's no wind in here."

She closed her eyes for a three count and focused

on containing her anger. As she passed the metal chair she'd done her interview in, she dragged it with her, scraping it loudly along the floor.

"Let me see," she murmured. She angled the clipboard on the leg of the chair and sat down, reached for Vyr.

He winced away. "I hate you seeing me like this."

"Is there audio?" she asked.

Vyr blinked those silver dragon eyes and murmured, "Not anymore."

"What happened?"

"Doesn't matter." His voice echoed with hollowness.

"Don't push me away."

"Riyah, it's best this way. I know what's coming. I can hear their thoughts so loud. And I'm tired. I've existed for thirty years with everyone thinking I'm evil. Doesn't matter the effort I put into keeping good people safe. I lost the dragon. Lost the biggest part of me, and now there's this hole. It's growing bigger and bigger, and now all I feel is..."

"Is what?"

"Emptiness."

Her lip quivered, so she sat back in the chair,

blinking hard because it wouldn't help Vyr if she cried right now.

"If everyone wants me gone so bad…okay. I don't really want to live a life where I feel like this anyway."

"What about me?" she asked. "I'll be alone if you leave. Really alone. I want more."

"More what?"

"Time. I want you to kiss me, hold my hand, take me out for coffee, and stay up all night talking while you're actually lying beside me. I've never felt this way about anyone before. It was instant for me. I should've been scared of you, right? Well, I wasn't. You always make me feel safe, even locked in here. I want to see Mr. Diddles and see your mountains. I want to be part of your crew. I want you to stick around because, to me, it doesn't matter if you have the dragon or not. To me, it only matters if you're here. With me. The princess and the dragon. A fairytale…except that's not us, is it? Not really. We were built in similar ways that made our edges too rough for anyone else to handle or they would get cut. But we don't cut each other. We fit. Now you go. What do you want?"

Vyr ran his hand over his cropped hair and then

leaned forward, grabbed her chair, and scooched her closer until her knees were between his thighs.

"No touching!" Emmitt said over the intercom.

Riyah flipped off his observation room, her gaze never leaving the exhausted lines of Vyr's face. "What do you want, Vyr?" she asked again.

"I want my dragon back. I want to be whole because I want to keep you."

God, what those words did to her insides. As she filled with warmth, she raised her hands, palms facing Vyr. He searched her eyes and then slid his much bigger hands against hers and then intertwined their fingers.

"I have a surprise for you," she whispered.

His ruddy eyebrows drew down. "What is it?"

"Come lay on the floor with me."

"Wait, are you wanting to fool around in here? We can."

"Dear lord, do all of your thoughts revolve around sex?"

"No. Yes. Look at your shirt! Your tits are all squished together, and I can see the edge of your bra. I wish I could push you against the wall and fuck you from behind until you're screaming my name."

Well, she needed to add that to her list of wants. Riyah offered a slow, drunken blink. "Hooooly wow." She cleared her throat once, twice. Opened her mouth but nothing intelligent came out. Just a soft gasp. Smooth. She cleared her throat once more and tried again. "Back to the surprise. Come on. I put a lot of work into this. Mostly because Emmitt is a stubborn anus and fought everything."

"What did you do?"

She laid down on the cold concrete right in the middle of the room and patted the space beside her. He limped over to her and laid down too, crossing his hands over his stomach.

Riyah smiled over at him and asked, "Are you ready?"

Vyr looked confused, but so handsome, staring unabashedly back at her, allowing her to look right into his frozen dragon eyes. He had a week of red facial scruff, and the freckles across his nose were stark. She'd never wanted to kiss a man so badly.

"I'm ready," he murmured in that deep voice of his.

Riyah closed her eyes and cut the lights. But she could still see him in the glow of the hundreds of plastic stars she'd taped to the ceiling. It had taken her hours to get it just right.

"Riyaaah," Vyr drawled out softly.

"Remember when you told me what you missed the most?"

"The sky. The stars."

"Yeah, and you said you liked to imagine them smiling down on you, even if you couldn't see them. And that they were smiling because they could see better things coming for you."

Vyr lay there unblinking up at the ceiling. "Yeah, I remember."

"Vyr. I'll be your star. I believe in you. I'll wait with you while better things are coming."

He stared up at the words she'd written with some of the stars. "I'm yours," he read aloud.

She smiled. "You just said you wanted the dragon back so you could keep me. Well...dragon or no, you have me."

Vyr slid his hand from his stomach and pulled her fingertips to his chest, right over his drumming heartbeat. He pressed her palm there and kept his hand on her like he didn't want her to pull away.

On a breath, she whispered, "You have me, so

trust me."

Any second, the guards would storm the room and ruin this, but this is what they had. Stolen moments. Stolen touches. And she didn't care what anyone thought. Only what Vyr thought. She didn't care about consequences or judgement. She cared about one thing—the man beside her, who was smiling...smiling despite everything that had been done to him.

He lifted two fingers up at the ceiling and whispered, "Look, Riyah."

The stars came off the ceiling and floated there above them, like real stars in the night sky. They rotated slowly, moving this way and that in different patterns until words formed. It was an I, a heart with a jagged crack down the middle, and a U. And as she watched in awe, the crack in the heart disappeared.

A tear slid from the corner of her eye down her cheek and made a tiny splat on the concrete.

Vyr rolled his head to the side and gave her a crooked smile. God, he was stunning, his dragon eyes glowing under the lights of the floating plastic stars, his smile for her certain, even though he must've been falling apart on the inside. "I feel steady around you."

"What do you mean?" she asked. "And where the hell are the guards?" She propped up on her elbows and stared at the observation room mirrors across the room. They should've been in here tearing her and Vyr apart about now, but no one had even knocked on the window and told them to cut it out.

"Oh, I put them all to sleep," Vyr said.

"W-what?"

"Oh, I can put people out. All the guards are on the floor right now. I made sure Emmitt hit his head on the way down because I can't fuckin' stand the way he talks to you." Vyr's smile turned wicked.

"Wait...you can put people out?"

"Yep. I can do a helluva lot people don't realize."

"Then what are you still doing in here?"

"I'm voluntary, Riyah."

"You lost your dragon on purpose?"

"No," he said without hesitation. "I didn't think they could actually take him. I believe in consequences, though. I burned a town. I've burned several towns, but I got busted in Covington. I saw Torren go headfirst into that fight with the gorillas and the Dunn lions. He was protecting his sister and his sister's crew, but I always have his back. So, I let the dragon have me. And I didn't even try to stop his rampage. I just…let him do what he wanted, consequences be damned. Then I ran to my mountains, and I started thinking. And I thought and thought and thought. And my dad was telling me I needed to listen to that one-year sentence. He wanted to smooth things over with the humans and keep peace between them and shifters. He's worked very hard to protect shifters. I understood why he wanted to give me up to the system. I hated it. Hated him for it. I wanted him to pick me over everyone else. Pick me over his precious crews, but the more I sat in my mountains, thinking, the more it made sense. The biggest change in me happened when Torren, Nox, and Nevada decided we were a crew, not just a dysfunctional group of friends thrown together. They made me alpha, and I'm shitty at it, but I don't want to be bad at this forever. I got this deep instinct to protect them. I loved…" Vyr swallowed hard, his muscular throat moving with it. "I love them. If I didn't come here and ride out my time, it would affect their whole lives. Our crew would always be on the run, always looking over our shoulders, and eventually they would get hurt protecting me. And that's not how it should be. I should be the one protecting them. This time in here makes me feel like I'm a better alpha because I put them first, before myself. Before my dragon. And now I understand why my dad wanted me in here. I can see how his protective instincts over all those people in his mountains, over all shifters, could drive him to give up his son. And especially if he thought he was teaching me a lesson like the one I'm learning."

"What lesson?"

"How to be a good alpha. And I know what I am. I am total destruction. I know what I'm capable of. I accepted it a long time ago. I had to. It was time for me to come here and pay the consequences for my actions. I will always miss the dragon." He cleared his throat and gave his attention back to the floating stars. "I'll never feel whole. There will always be a huge part of me missing, and I will live a half-life. I'll always hate the people here for what they did. I'll fight bitterness for the rest of my life. I'll fight the emptiness. I won't have a single easy day because every time I look in the mirror, I'm going to hurt. There's no accepting the loss of my dragon, but I had to do this. For my crew."

"Vyr," she whispered, her voice breaking. She wished more than anything that she could fix his life. She had this vision of him staring in the mirror and slamming his fist against the glass, over and over, and in each frame he aged until he was gray and tired, and still, he hated his frozen dragon eyes. She was going to watch the man she loved break every day because of what happened here.

"I like what you're wearing today," Vyr murmured.

She looked down at her dark wash jeans, sneakers, and plain, black, fitted, cotton T-shirt. She'd dressed it up with cute turquoise jewelry, but it was the most casual thing she'd worn since she started working for the prison. "Emmitt called my high heels victim shoes, and lately it feels like I need to be ready."

"For what?"

"For total destruction," she said with a smile.

"I should tell you I'm not a good man. I stole a lot of things from you without you knowing. Sometimes I spend time with you in your head when you don't realize it. Quietly. Picking through memories.

Learning about you."

"Why do you do that?"

"Because I can't get enough of you. I want to know everything. You're so light. So optimistic, so beautiful inside and outside. I like everything about you. Even the things you're ashamed of. I like that your favorite color is rainbow." He chuckled. "Whose favorite color is all of them?"

She snorted. "Mine."

"And I like that you eat a carton of chocolate chip cookie dough when you're upset and that you're fine with boxes all over your house, which is insane because I'm extremely tidy. But I imagine you leaving your shit all over my house and how it'll make me feel."

"How will it make you feel?"

"Like you're everywhere. Like you're filling up all the space that used to be boring. I think a week with you, and I'll have trouble remembering my old life."

Her stomach fluttered. She slid over to him, pressed right against his ribs, and rested her cheek on the inside of his shoulder. He was looking at her with that same crooked smile she couldn't get enough of.

"What else did you learn while you were being a memory thief?"

"That you want kids, but you're afraid they would have your powers."

"Yeah, well now I'm double concerned because you have, like, eight guards in comas, and with very little effort."

"And I've turned off all the cameras for the entire lower level. One hundred percent, any babies I put in you would be little hellions. But...they would also be good. You know how I know?"

"How?" she asked softly.

"Because you would be their mother. And I can see you so clearly, Riyah. You told me once that you're the monster, but you were wrong. You're good."

"A good witch," she teased.

And he agreed. "A very good witch."

Vyr lifted up and rolled her onto her back, cupped her cheek as he searched her eyes. Riyah gripped his wrist to keep him touching her like this. Above him the glowing stars were still rotating slowly. It was amazing the things he could control all at once when he didn't even look like he was focusing on them.

His lips curved into a smile just as he leaned down and pressed them to hers. It was so different from their first kiss, which was rushed and violent, and his hand had been so rough on her leg. This one was love, not lust. It was tender. It was soft sipping and steady breathing and lips moving together. When he brushed his tongue against her bottom lip, she opened for him. He didn't taste like smoke anymore, and there was a moment when that made her sad, but she squeezed her eyes closed and focused on enjoying their time together because they might not get this again. Vyr dragged his fingertips down her ribs to her hip, gripped her, and pulled her against him with a deep, sexy sound in his throat. His touch was fire, blazing against her skin as he slid his hand up her shirt. He pushed under her bra and gripped her breast so hard she gasped and her back arched on reflex.

"Mmmm, good girl," he rumbled.

Okay, now her body was igniting. Vyr shoved her shirt up over her head and ripped her bra off. Ripped it, not unfastened. His hands were firm and steady as he sat up and pulled her with him. He sat back and yanked his shirt over his head. "Skin. I want to feel your skin," he demanded.

Oh God, she'd never liked being told what to do, but hell yes to Vyr taking control. She kicked out of her shoes and shimmied out of her pants as he watched. She planned on straddling him but he caught her by the hips, settled her upright on locked legs, and eased onto his knees before she could move. His fingers dug into her waist as he held her still and licked her right between the thighs...slowly. With a gasp, she locked her arms against his shoulders, because she wasn't going to stay upright for this, she could already tell. Her legs were going numb.

He sucked gently on her clit, brushing his tongue against it rhythmically until she was panting and digging her nails into his shoulders. And then right when she was on the verge of orgasm, he thrust his tongue deep inside her until she was throbbing hard. She panted his name, legs buckling, but he had her, held her upright. And then he trailed biting kisses up her stomach to her breasts as he lowered her slowly to his lap. When he sucked hard on her nipple, she cupped his head and tossed her head back, closed her eyes, and melted into his touch. When she finally settled onto his lap, his erection was hard against her sex. Vyr slid his arms around her and pulled her against his chest, as if he was just testing his strength, testing how much pressure she could take. Her back cracked and her breath left her lungs with a needy sound. He gripped her ass as he thrust his hips against her.

Riyah lifted up enough to shove his pants down his hips, unsheathing his thick, hard dick. That was hers. When she rocked against him, Vyr closed his eyes and huffed a breath. He reached between them and grabbed his dick, poised it right at her entrance. Riyah slid over him, slowly, focused on relaxing so she could take all of him, and when she had, she rocked faster. It felt so good, having him move inside of her, being connected like this. Vyr spread his knees farther apart and slammed into her, meeting her, moving with her, fingers rough on her hips as he kept her on him. He pushed into her harder and faster until she was chanting his name, and just as her second orgasm blasted through her, Vyr clamped his teeth on her neck and groaned, thrust deep, and throbbed warmth into her. He didn't break the skin, but his bite felt so good as her release pulsed on and on. They moved together, drawing every aftershock from each other's bodies. And when they were spent and still at last, she cupped his cheeks and smiled. "That was..." What word could she possibly use to describe something so important?

"For me, too," he murmured. Vyr pulled her in close and hugged her tight. "It's not exactly the way I wanted it for us, though."

She giggled. "You mean you didn't have prison sex in mind when you started wooing me?"

Vyr snorted and tickled her ribs until she squirmed, then laid them down on the concrete and pulled her against his side. With a sigh, he looked up at the floating stars and murmured, "Thank you for tonight, Riyah. For giving me the sky for a little while."

With a content sigh, she kissed his chest, right over his heart, and nuzzled her cheek against him. "Someday, I'm going to give you the real thing." It was a promise she was making to him and to herself. She was going to figure this out because she couldn't watch him hate his reflection forever. There had to be something better than a half-life for Vyr.

In this moment, she didn't care what would happen to her if she found a way to save the Red

Dragon.

In this moment, she didn't care about the fire that Beaston had promised.

In this moment, Riyah realized, as long as Vyr existed on this Earth, she would never be in the dark again. And as long as she existed, neither would he.

# FIFTEEN

Riyah's burner phone rang just as she was driving into the prison parking lot. In a rush, she pulled into a spot crooked and fumbled around in her purse until she found it.

"Hello?" she answered, hoping she hadn't missed it.

"Turn on the news," was all Damon Daye said before the line went dead.

Okay then. She'd been in lala land, aka thinking about Vyr-diddles the entire drive here, and now she was jolted back to reality. She pulled out her personal cell phone and connected to the internet. Well, news footage on Vyr wasn't hard to find. Every link she clicked showed video of somber anchors talking about the death of the Red Dragon at the hands of the New IESA.

*...against his will...*

*...not what our prison system should've been doing...*

*...grotesque use of power...*

*...the dragon is finally incapacitated...*

*...the world is a safer place...*

*...horrified by the secrecy...*

*...apparently the International Exchange of Shifter Affairs has been revived, to the detriment of all shifter-kind...*

*...the New IESA...*

*...experiments on shifters...*

*...a second look at shifter rights in the prison system...*

*...dragon is dead...*

*...dead...*

*...dead...*

*...the Red Dragon is dead...*

Feeling sick, Riyah clicked on the video with the most views. It had been released late last night and already had several million hits. It opened with shaky footage of the conversation with Emmitt. Well, shit.

She was the only one in the room when they had that conversation. She was definitely busted as the rat.

"Fuck," she muttered as her heart rate went to racing and the blood drained out of her face and hands so quickly her skin tingled. Why would Cora Keller and Beck Anderson blast this out there? They'd completely blown her cover, and she wasn't done here yet. Vyr was still in here, still at risk. She struggled to hold the phone steady as she watched the rest of the video.

The entire conversation between her and Emmitt was on there, and then the screen faded to black. Words typed across the darkness as Vyr said, "I hate you seeing me like this."

The screen morphed to Vyr, running his hand down his short beard, his scar an angry red from his temple to the back of his head. She wasn't in the scene, but her voice rang out clearly. "What happened?"

"Doesn't matter." His voice sounded so defeated, and he ghosted a glance at the camera, flashing those sad, frozen dragon eyes.

"Don't push me away," she pleaded.

"Riyah, it's best this way. I know what's coming."

The scene faded to black, and words started typing across the dark again as Vyr spoke. "I'm tired. I've existed for thirty years with everyone thinking I'm evil. Doesn't matter the effort I put into keeping good people safe. I lost the dragon. Lost the biggest part of me, and now there's this hole. It's growing bigger and bigger, and now all I feel is..."

"Is what?" she murmured.

"Emptiness." Vyr's voice echoed with sadness. The video showed Vyr again, and he was looking down at his clenched hands between his knees, shaking his head as he uttered, "If everyone wants me gone so bad...okay. I don't really want to live a life where I feel like this anyway."

"What about me?" Riyah asked from offscreen. "I'll be alone if you leave. Really alone. I want more."

"More what?"

"Time. I want you to kiss me, hold my hand, take me out for coffee, and stay up all night talking while you're actually lying beside me. I've never felt this way about anyone before. It was instant for me. I should've been scared of you, right? Well, I wasn't. You always make me feel safe, even locked in here. I want to see Mr. Diddles and see your mountains. I want to be part of your crew. I want you to stick around because, to me, it doesn't matter if you have the dragon or not. To me, it only matters if you're here. With me. The princess and the dragon. A fairytale...except that's not us, is it? Not really. We were built in similar ways that made our edges too rough for anyone else to handle or they would get cut. But we don't cut each other. We fit. Now you go. What do you want?"

Vyr ran his hand over his hair roughly and then leaned forward, grabbed her chair, and pulled her close. The camera changed angles, aiming at both of them as they stared into each other's eyes.

"What do you want, Vyr?" she asked.

"I want my dragon back. I want to be whole because I want to keep you."

Riyah put her hands up, and then Vyr slid his much bigger hands against hers and intertwined their fingers.

"I have a surprise for you," she whispered.

He frowned. "What is it?"

"Come lay on the floor with me."

The scene cut to a shot of the cement ceiling, covered in black scorch marks. The words appeared on the screen as she and Vyr spoke. "Are you ready?" she asked.

"I'm ready," Vyr answered.

The lights cut suddenly, and the scene was just pitch black with hundreds of plastic glowing stars. And their words appearing in closed captions.

"Riyaaah."

"Remember when you told me what you missed the most?"

"The sky. The stars."

"Yeah, and you said you liked to imagine them smiling down on you, even if you couldn't see them. And that they were smiling because they could see better things coming for you."

"Yeah, I remember."

"Vyr. I'll be your star. I believe in you. I'll wait with you while better things are coming."

"I'm yours," he read aloud.

There was a pause, and then in an emotional voice, Riyah murmured, "You just said you wanted the dragon back so you could keep me. Well...dragon or no, you have me."

Slowly, the glowing stars faded to black.

And just like that, whoever had edited this video

had humanized the most misunderstood shifter in the world. They had turned him from monster to man.

The scene cut to a pair of news anchors. A pretty blond woman was dabbing her eyes with a Kleenex, and the man asked if she was okay.

"Yes, yes, I'm fine, it's just sad. Shifters really and truly are people, with feelings and fears and hopes and dreams just like humans. When my crew and my husband, Boone, were coming out to the public all those years ago, it was so scary for us. It was terrifying. We were scared for our families, and now it feels like that's been revived. That fear of shifters. And because of that fear, you have these underground, secret operations that pop up and experiment on shifters, abuse them, torture them, steal their animals, and who is holding them accountable? Who? Whose place is it to stand up and say it's not right what they are doing?"

"The public," the man answered somberly.

The woman—*Cora Keller,* the name read along the bottom of the screen—turned to the camera, and her voice went steely as she said, "I agree. It's up to us to stop experimentation and involuntary cleansing of shifter animals. The suicide rate of shifters who have been cleansed is horrifying. I want the New IESA brought down. I want it annihilated, and I think we should revisit Vyr Daye spending another six months of his sentence in that godforsaken place. The government already seized all his assets, and he has paid to rebuild Covington, and now his dragon has been tortured to death. *To death.* I think he's suffered enough. I've started a petition online. You can find it at www-dot-stop-the-new-IESA-dot-com. Join me and thousands of others in making a positive change."

Cora continued talking, but Riyah turned off the phone and stared in shock out the front window. Well, that was one way to do it. Too bad it was still up to her to keep Vyr and Nox and Torren protected on the inside of that prison until a decision about Vyr's sentence could be reached.

"Vyr?" she asked. He'd been quiet all morning, and that hadn't bothered her because it was early, and she'd thought he was probably still sleeping. Now alarms were blaring inside her head though, and this newfound feeling of uneasiness just wouldn't go away.

"Vyr?" she tried again, but she was met with silence.

"Shoot," she murmured, grabbing her purse and clipboard. She faced the gold star toward her and said, "Something feels wrong, and I'm so busted they probably won't let me in the prison, but I have to try. Damon, you said I could have the crews if I needed them. That I'm not alone? Well...I have a really bad feeling, and I think I need help."

Riyah slid out of her Xterra and slammed the door, then bolted for the prison entrance, grateful she'd had the foresight to wear sneakers again today. When she made it through the first security checkpoint with nothing more than a harried, "Hurry up, it's chaos in there," from one of the new daytime guards, Riyah was shocked. She'd been sure they would stop her from even getting this far. Okay, one check-point at a time.

The second and third went off without a hitch too, but when she got inside the prison walls, the new guard had been right—it was utter chaos. Rows of inmates were chained at the ankles and wrists in neat lines, waiting to leave through the transportation doors.

"What's happening?" she asked Euless, who was hanging against the back wall, watching the guards yell orders to the inmates.

"You sure do know how to make an entrance, don't you?" he asked. He gestured toward the masses. "All them boys have been pumped full of meds to keep them from shifting and they are being transported to different shifter prisons."

"Different ones? Why?"

"Because you got this one shut down. I'm pretty damn impressed. Except now I'm out of a job, so thanks for that."

"You deserve better than to be mopping up peas after grown men anyway."

"Yep, I do." He lowered his voice. "I ain't seen a soul from the lower levels. I've been watching for 'em. See that lady guard over there?" He jerked his chin toward a stout blonde with a nametag that read *Tominson*. "She's one of ours, and she just told me the lower levels ain't even on the transportation lists."

"What does that mean?" she whispered.

"I can't be for certain, but I'm guessing it means they're gettin' rid of evidence." Euless's bushy brows jacked up to his hairline. "You better hurry."

"Oh, my gosh, okay. Thanks, Euless." She strode away as fast as she could without drawing attention, but no one stopped her as she made her way to the elevator that would take her to the lower levels. However, when she swiped her card into the reader, it read *ERROR*.

"Oh no. No, no, come on," she muttered, swiping it again with the same result.

Three more times got three more error messages, and now she was panicking. She needed to find someone with lower level clearance right freaking now. But when she turned to track down someone to help, she ran into a solid wall of muscle. Hank Butted gripped her arms. At first, she thought he was steadying her with those cold, clammy hands of his, but then he swiped his card and shoved her into the elevator with him before she could even protest.

Horrified, she backed into the opposite corner of the small space. The lights dimmed and the elevator slowed with the power that pulsed from her. Fear did that.

"Settle down, witch. I'm not going to kill you. And you're welcome. The New IESA doesn't like spies, and I'm getting you down to the action. That's where you want to be…right? Front row seat to the show?"

"W-what show?"

"They're going to kill Vyr's crew in front of him…and then they're going to kill Vyr. And I'm gonna love watching your face when they do it."

The power surged and the elevator dipped so fast her stomach lurched.

"Steady, witch. I'm not the one you're after. I'm here to witness, just like you."

She trusted him about as far as she could throw him though, so she remained plastered to the wall as he strode out of the elevator. With a steadying breath, she followed him out, but Butte rounded on her so suddenly he blurred. And then he slammed a needle into the side of her neck as he smiled like a demon. "Gotcha."

Riyah's legs buckled, but he held her upright and dragged her down the hallway, singing "ding-dong, the witch is dead," in a gravelly, off-key voice.

She was having trouble controlling her body, and her legs wouldn't hold her weight. "Don't worry, I'll get you fixed up in no time," he murmured as they reached Vyr's lair. He swiped his card into the two entryways. And as he dragged her into the sprawling room with the scorch marks and plastic stars that had fallen all over the floor, he whispered in her ear,

"I wasn't lying when I told you I wasn't going to kill you. Not right away at least. First, I want to give you something worse than death."

He turned her in his arms, and there were Vyr, Nox, and Torren, looking like they'd been through ten rounds of a boxing match, on their knees, hands cuffed behind their backs.

"No," Vyr growled through a split lip.

"Don't worry," Butte sang. "She made it just in time."

"Worse than death," she slurred.

"That's right, Witch. I'm going to Turn you." Without another second of warning, Butte opened his mouth and sank his teeth into the side of her neck. Pain blasted through her, the arms of the burn spreading from where his teeth pierced her skin downward. He released her just as she screamed at the fiery pain, and he said, "Now you're one of the things that killed your dad. Enjoy the bear while you can."

The roaring in her ears drowned out everything. Warmth trickled down the side of her neck, and time slowed to a crawl as she fell to her knees, tear-filled eyes on the Sons of Beasts. Nox and Torren were fighting the hand-cuffs, yelling something at her she couldn't understand. And Vyr…her Vyr…was glaring behind her at Butte with the promise of death in his blue eyes. There were a dozen guards with their weapons trained on Riyah, Vyr, Nox, and Torren, but all she could hear was Butte's laughter behind her.

Emmitt was giving an order. What order? He was jamming his finger at Vyr, and the guards aimed.

No. No, no, no, this wasn't Vyr's fate. Better things were coming. They had to be.

She needed fire. She needed Damon and Dark Kane. She needed Roe, Harper, and Diem to rain hell down on this place and save them, but they weren't here. They hadn't made it in time.

She needed dragon's fire.

Fire.

The Red Dragon had fire.

Everyone was yelling—everyone but Vyr. He was looking right at her.

*"Can you feel it?"*

"Feel w-what?" she asked, tears streaming down her cheeks as she resisted curling around the pain in her middle. Something awful was growing inside of her.

*"Look at me. Really look."*

She did, but Vyr was blurry. His edges were too soft, and there was a smoke-gray fog rolling from him into her.

*"Take it, Riyah. Take it and get out of here. Everything is going to be okay."*

It was those last words that snapped her out of it. Mom had said that too, and it hadn't been okay. It hadn't. She'd lost too much, and she would be good-goddamned if she lost Vyr and his crew, too.

Red Dragon.

Fire. Fire everywhere.

And it hit her what she was supposed to do.

No more hating his reflection. No more broken mirrors. No more frozen silver eyes.

No. More. Half-life.

The New IESA owed Vyr a dragon.

Closing her eyes, she reached out with her mind, down the hallway to the lab. In through the doors, through the maze of tables, past the lab equipment and to the room they'd locked up tight. The room where they kept the dragon-in-a-syringe. Power throbbed from her skin. She was bloated with it thanks to Vyr dumping his into her. She smiled as she touched the metal canister that held Vyr's future.

Fuck consequences.

She lifted her hand into the air and pulled with all her power. The crashing sounds were deafening, and the cavernous room shook. When she opened her eyes, Vyr was dropping guards. One by one, they were going limp, slamming against the concrete. Butte roared a challenge behind her, and Emmitt was screaming orders, but she couldn't take her eyes from the building fury in Vyr's face. With one last twitch of her hand, Riyah pulled a hole through the cement and steel rebar. The banged-up canister slammed onto the ground and skidded right to Vyr.

Shocked, he looked down at it. "What are you doing?" he asked.

Her body hurt so bad. Sooo bad. She was breaking from the inside out as a smattering of pops sounded. Were those her bones? Through clenched teeth, she gritted out, "I'm giving you the sky." And then such agonizing pain rippled through her she couldn't do more than lay there on the cold concrete and stare helplessly at the man she loved.

There was a single second of hesitation before Vyr turned to Torren and Nox. "Change now! Protect

Riyah!" He twitched his fingers and the metal canister ripped away and a single syringe fell to the concrete.

Emmitt was running for it, so close, but Vyr held out his hand, and the tiny needle-capped vial snapped into his palm as fast as a bullet. And in one smooth motion, he slammed it into his arm as he smiled wickedly at Butte. "Run," he snarled. "Run like the devil's behind you. Because he is."

And then the massive red dragon exploded from Vyr's body. A suffocating wave of power pulsed from him and the walls blasted outward. His Firestarter clicked, and the dragon aimed, and spewed a stream of fire. Butte and Emmitt's screams filled her head. She didn't even want to see. Nox's blond grizzly was sprinting for her, followed closely by Torren's massive silverback. They reached her just as rubble rained down, and covered her body with theirs.

Flames devoured everything, and the heat blistered her skin. She squeezed her eyes closed and didn't open them again until her skin cooled. There was nothing left but Vyr, Nox, Torren, her, and piles of ashes covering the floor.

Why wasn't her body working? Was it the drugs Butte had given her? Or was it her inability to control the enormous white paws with six-inch, curved, razor-sharp black claws that had replaced her blunt human hands? Was her body broken because of the animal? Because of the bear? Or was this what it was like to be frozen in terror?

Beaston and his son had been right. There was fire everywhere. Vyr was indeed total destruction. He stretched his ripped-up, blood-red wings, shielding her and Nox and Torren from the debris that fell from the ceiling as he arched his massive, red-scaled head back and opened his jaws, spraying magma at the roof.

"Fuck," Torren said in a growling, inhuman voice. "We need to move. He's gonna level this place."

He shoved Riyah out from under a massive chunk of ceiling that shattered on the floor with a plume of dust. Light filled the room, and above them, Vyr had blasted a huge hole in the prison to expose the sky. It wasn't big enough for him to escape. Or so she thought, but just as Torren gripped the scruff of her neck to pull her away, Vyr roared, bunched his muscles, and rocketed up into the sky like an enormous crimson missile, the walls of the prison exploding outward as he escaped his hell.

"Vyr, no!" Torren bellowed. But it was too late. The Red Dragon was pissed, and now he was free to unleash hell on earth as he saw fit.

But far above, just as he reached the clouds, a blue dragon locked onto him with his claws, and both spewed fire and snapped at each other. Damon.

Something monstrous and black flew over the opening of the destroyed prison. Dark Kane was here and so was Roe's dark silver dragon and the two green dragons, Harper and Diem.

If Riyah knew how to cry from relief in this body, she would have. The dragons weren't here to hurt Vyr. They were herding him toward the west, taking turns swooping in. Pushing him. Taking hits from his fire and refusing to burn him back.

Outside, the roars and snarls, calls and caws of countless animals filled the air. Beside her, Nox roared and Torren beat his chest loudly, like a war drum. And then something happened, something deep within her. Rocked to her core and shocked at all that had happened, she answered the call of her new people. She struggled to her feet, lifted her head to the sky, and screamed. Only it didn't sound like her voice anymore scratching up the back of her throat.

Instead, a bellowing roar shook up from her chest and rattled the ground beneath her massive paws.

Tomorrow would have to take care of itself. She would have to learn how to be this new creature, and she would have to accept all that had happened. Her future had just been thrown into chaos, but really, that had begun long before now. It had happened the day she saw Vyr. She hadn't been born for a steady, easy, normal life. Neither had her mate. But right now, she wanted to celebrate the victories.

Vyr was still alive.

The Red Dragon was still alive, and the man she loved was whole.

Nox and Torren stood strong beside her, and somewhere out there in the woods that surrounded the prison, she knew Nevada and Candace were with the rest of the shifters of Damon's Mountains, Kane's Mountains, and Harper's Mountains.

Damon had been right. She hadn't been alone.

Riyah wanted to cry and scream and laugh and yell and roar with the relief that wracked her body in waves.

She'd heard it many times and uttered it herself, but this...right now...was the first time she'd ever felt it to be true.

Everything was going to be okay.

# EPILOGUE

Vyr slid his hand over Riyah's thigh just to feel her. The dragon felt steadier now, but only when she was right beside him. She didn't realize the power she had over him.

His life wasn't dark and hopeless anymore. Big changes had begun the day his crew had decided he would be their alpha, and it had turned around completely the day Riyah decided he was hers to save.

"What's the surprise?" she asked. But her voice quivered with excitement, and he glanced over at her to find her cheeks flushed and her eyes the bright blue of her polar bear. Beautiful mate. Snow white fur when she was Changed, and eyes that stayed the color of frost now while she learned to control the animal. She was a warrior when Nox felt like fighting another bear. One month moved into his mansion, and she was already gaining control of her Changes with the patient guidance of Nevada and Candace. He loved watching her with the girls. She fit in with them, and took care of them, had their backs like they had hers.

"I'm so damn proud of you," he murmured.

"For not guessing the surprise?" she asked, her dark eyebrows furrowing.

"No, I mean, I'm proud that you're mine. Proud you're my mate. Proud you picked me back. Me. Who am I? A damaged dragon, but you're good and powerful—"

"A polar bear witch," she teased.

"My dad fell for a bear shifter, and now look at me. Dragons and bears," he said and huffed a laugh. "I'm lucky."

"We're lucky," she murmured, smiling at him so sweetly. God, he loved her. Loved her with everything he had because this woman smiling at him from the passenger's side of his truck had dragged him out of the shadows and made his life manageable. No.

Manageable wasn't a big enough word for what she'd done.

She'd made his life happy, and hopeful.

He pulled through the last of the trees into the clearing around the old sawmill where he'd set up Riyah's surprise. But where he'd expected to see the dilapidated and abandoned sawmill he'd bought for Torren all those years ago, the weed-riddled grounds in front of it were covered with people.

And not just any people. People he recognized. People he'd quietly loved all his life.

The Ashe Crew, the Gray Backs, the Breck Crew, the Lowlanders, the Boarlanders, the Boodrunners, Blackwings, Red Havoc, and lastly…his Sons of Beasts.

"What the hell?" he murmured in shock as he pulled to a stop in front of the crowd.

"I know you meant to bring me here for a surprise, but I had one for you, too."

"You did this?" he asked.

Her eyes were already full of tears, and he ran the pad of his thumb across her cheek as one slipped down. "What's wrong?"

"I know it must've been so hard growing up and feeling people's fear of you. Growing up different and never feeling like you fit in. And I know the dragon is still hard to manage. I watch you struggle with Changes, Torren's overprotectiveness of you, and Nox's stress when he tries to stop your Changes. I know it might always be like this, but..." She swallowed hard, pulled his hand to her cheek, and rubbed it against his palm. "People care about you, Vyr Daye. You got thousands of shifters to rally behind you and get your sentence reduced. You have the devotion of your crew, and they look up to you, to the alpha you've become, and I'm so proud. You never complained about how tough it was for you. You managed the strain silently and without the desire for any attention. You protected those you could. You, Vyr, are really good at this alpha gig."

"You make me want to be even better," he admitted low. "And I think that says something good when a person makes you want to be better."

Movement caught his eye, and Vyr narrowed his eyes at Nox, who was standing over a grill and dangling a long bratwurst from a pair of tongs. He wore the biggest shit-eating grin, along with short shorts, yellow and white tube socks, and a trucker hat that said *my balls are bigger than your balls*.

"Huh," Vyr murmured. He scratched his short beard with his thumbnail and wondered aloud, "What is Nox cooking?"

"He spent the electric bill money this month to pay the butcher for custom two-foot-long sausages for this shindig. We're at serious risk of having the power cut off, but at least he can tell a bunch of dick jokes now."

"Soooo many dick jokes are about to happen."

"He also painted the sign," she muttered, nodding her chin toward a hideous highlighter-yellow sign with pink writing. *Vyr, Vyr Needs Six Beers. Poet as fuck. MVP Goes to Nox. Nox FULLER in Case You Fuckers Were Confused. Eat my bratwurst.*

"He came up with the name of this party himself. Then he and Torren got in a huge fight, and Torren shot him through the calf with a crossbow. Nevada Changed into her fox and nearly ate the baby swans, and Candace's newest pregnancy craving is olives dipped in peanut butter for breakfast." Riyah pursed her lips against a pretty smile. "It's been an eventful morning."

He nodded his head in agreeance, but it sounded just about like every other morning to Vyr. As long as he lived, he would never take for granted the antics of his crew. He used to get so angry with their behavior, but then he'd spent six months away from them and missed the hell out of this place.

He shoved his door open, and Riyah met him at the front of the truck. They were swarmed by the crews. He kept looking back at Riyah as they were pulled into hugs. He lost track of how many people touched him, but as he was passed from person to person, something shifted inside of him. And he began to hug them back, hesitantly at first, but then it got easier and easier until he made it to his parents.

Mom was already crying. She looked so happy, red hair the same shade as his, shining in the sun, tears streaking down her cheeks, her arm linked in Riyah's. Tears had always confused him. Mom was saying something to his mate and it was making the tears come faster. To try and understand, Vyr scratched at Riyah's thoughts.

Mom was thanking her for bringing her son back.

Her son? But the dragon was separate. She'd never lost Vyr, just the Red Dragon for a day.

And when he switched to his mother's thoughts, he was overwhelmed. He could feel her love for him.

And not just the human side, but all of him. She'd always believed in him and his ability to become the man he was. He balked at her thoughts because his heart felt strange. It felt like it had swelled too big for his chest. There was a dull ache. And as he looked around at all the crews of Damon's Mountains and beyond, he thought perhaps he hadn't been the outcast he'd imagined.

Why else would they all come to his aid at the prison? Why orchestrate a nation-wide rally in his defense? Why would the dragons keep him from scorching the earth? Why would they pledge to help keep him out of trouble every three weeks when he had to Change?

*"Because you are very loved, Vyr,"* Riyah whispered, the words rattling around in his head. Her emotional gaze went to something behind him, and when Vyr turned, his father was standing there, stoic as always, his dark hair gone silver at the temples, his white oxford shirt and gray suit pants perfectly crisp. His eyes though…those were silver, and his Adam's apple moved as he swallowed hard. "I don't always make the right decisions."

"You don't have to explain—"

"I do. Wanting you to serve that sentence…it was never about choosing anyone over you, Vyr. Not the humans, not shifters. You're my boy. My pride and joy. From the moment I held you, I was so damn proud to have you as my son, and I swore I was going to be a good father for you. If they killed the dragon…" His voice faded, and he lurched toward Vyr, pulled him into a tight hug, clenching his shirt with his fists. "If they had succeeded, I would've never forgiven myself. Your dragon isn't a monster. I hope you know that. He reminds me so much of my own dragon, but when I was young, we had wars that quenched that thirst to burn everything. I was hard on you about controlling the Red Dragon, but I sometimes forget what it's like for you, having so many eyes on you and having that pressure to be perfect all the time. I don't want you to be perfect. I want you to be happy." Damon released his shirt, clapped him on the back roughly and then took a step away, slid his arm around his mate, who was looking back and forth between Vyr and Damon with the mushiest smile.

Vyr's stupid eyes were leaking, and he needed to get out of here. "I need a moment with my mate." He turned to leave, but changed his mind and uttered the words he felt before he chickened out. "I love you, Dad."

"I love you too, Son," Damon murmured through a slow-growing smile.

Now mom was bawling, so Vyr blew out a breath and nodded to Torren as he passed. His best friend gave him an are-you-okay-and-who-do-I-need-to-fuck-up look, but Vyr shook his head slightly. He would tell him all about that little moment when he had time to sit of the roof of the mansion and think on everything.

He grabbed Riyah by the hand and pulled her toward the edge of the old sawmill. And when they rounded the corner, he scooped her up in a hug and kissed her just to feel steady again. He walked with her like that, holding her, listening to her happy thoughts, absorbing her devotion and love until there was no darkness left in him. Oh, it would come back. The darkness would always come back, but Riyah was light and she never dimmed. She gave and gave, selflessly and without realizing. Not even the apex predator inside of her had dampened her caring nature.

She was hugging his neck so tight, legs wrapped around his waist, completely focused on him, and that had been the plan. Distraction. Because he really did have a surprise for her.

Slowly, Vyr lowered her to the ground and kissed her in little smacks, one, two, three, four. "Remember when you gave me the sky?" he asked her low, swimming in those pretty blue eyes of hers.

"Yes," she whispered.

Vyr gripped her shoulders gently and turned her toward the orchard of peach trees he'd spent the last three days planting.

"Oh, my gosh," she whispered, drawing her hands to her face as she scanned the rows of fruit trees. "You planted these for me?" Her voice shook.

"It's the least I could do," he said, sliding his arms around her chest and resting his chin on top of her hair. "Thank you for seeing in me what no one took the time to. You kept me fighting in that prison. And then you saved me. You didn't just give me the sky, Riyah." He kissed the top of her head and imagined their future stretching on and on. "You gave me everything."

It wasn't the mountains that were Vyr's treasure.

It wasn't freedom. It wasn't even the crew.

It was Riyah, the light-giver and banisher of soul shadows.

Riyah the witch.

Riyah the polar bear shifter.

Riyah the mate of the Red Dragon.

His Riyah of the Sons of Beasts Crew.

He'd never really been alone, but it took meeting her to realize that. Because of her, he was back in his mountains. Because of her, the dragon lived. Because of her, he had a future, a crew, a home, and a place in this world where people weren't afraid of him.

Because of her love, Vyr would never be in the dark again.

# SON OF THE DRAGON

# Want more of these characters?

Son of the Dragon is the third and final book in the Sons of Beasts series.

For more of these characters, check out these other books from T. S. Joyce.

**Son of the Cursed Bear**
(Sons of Beasts, Book 1)

**Son of Kong**
(Sons of Beasts, Book 2)

This is a spinoff series set in the Damon's Mountains universe. Start with Lumberjack Werebear to enjoy the very beginning of this adventure.

## About the Author

T.S. Joyce is devoted to bringing hot shifter romances to readers. Hungry alpha males are her calling card, and the wilder the men, the more she'll make them pour their hearts out. She werebear swears there'll be no swooning heroines in her books. It takes tough-as-nails women to handle her shifters.

She lives in a tiny town, outside of a tiny city, and devotes her life to writing big stories. Foodie, wolf whisperer, ninja, thief of tiny bottles of awesome smelling hotel shampoo, nap connoisseur, movie fanatic, and zombie slayer, and most of this bio is true.

Bear Shifters? Check

Smoldering Alpha Hotness? Double Check

Sexy Scenes? Fasten up your girdles, ladies and gents, it's gonna to be a wild ride.

For more information on T. S. Joyce's work,
visit her website at
www.tsjoyce.com

Printed in Great Britain
by Amazon